MW00916508

THE LEGEND OF CRYSTAL FALLS

VIOLET NOEL

This book is a work of fiction. Names, characters, companies, organizations, places, events, locales, and incidents are fictional or used in a fictitious manner. Any resemblance to actual persons, living or dead, actual companies or organizations, or actual events is coincidental.

Copyright © 2022 by Violet Noel

All rights reserved. No portion of this book may be reproduced in any form without written permission of the author, except as permitted by U.S. copyright law.

~ To an amazing theater director ~

"It's amazing what young people can do when given the opportunity."

-James Hart

OLIVER - THE PREMONITION

"Run!"

I clutched desperately to a girl's hand as we dashed through the forest. Branches of trees tugged and tore at my jeans and T-shirt as if urging me to let go of her hand and stay there... but I couldn't. A loud roar rend the air as we continued running. Birds took flight from the safety of the trees, flying over our heads. The sky was turning blood red, as if a drop of red paint had dripped onto a painter's masterpiece, seeping slowly and deliberately through the bends and folds of the wet paint. The wind howled and whipped around us. A fallen branch caught my foot, and I collapsed on the earthy floor. My foot felt like someone had sawed it off. I looked behind to see if my foot was still there when the girl, I somehow knew her name, Cora, ran over and knelt down next to me. She touched my foot, and a stabbing pain went through me. I yelled.

"It must be broken!"

"Obviously!" I yelled at her, "What are we going to do! He's right behind us!"

Cora turned as faint laughter slowly grew louder and the world around us was turning black. Trees were rotting as black vines curved around their trunks and throttled their roots.

"Oliver! Give me your hand!"

"What!?!"

"Do you trust me?"

I stared hard into her electric blue eyes, trying to understand why she wanted me to take her hand at a time like this. Until now, I hadn't realized that her eyes had golden flecks on the outer edge of her pupils. Finally, I nodded. She smiled and reached out for my hand.

A blast of magenta black fire missed Cora's ear by a mere millimeter. A tall, shadowy man emerged from the darkness. He wore a long, black trench coat, with black leather gloves, and a black hat that was angled off to the right to show only half of his face. The only side of his face that we could see was as pale as a sheet of paper, and he had an eye that was pure black with a magenta pupil.

"It's over, daughter of Delphi," the man said with a voice that didn't match his physique. "Give up now... And no one *else* will get hurt."

I stared at Cora.

Delphi? Who is Delphi?

Cora looked at the man, and I swear on my life that I had never seen such hatred etched in anyone's face like that before.

"I'd rather die, Malice!" she hollered.

The man, or Malice apparently, flexed his fingers and stepped forward.

"I can arrange that."

An orb of magenta black fire formed in his hands. He raised his right arm and then slashed downward. The fire barreled towards us. Cora grabbed my hand and together in a flash of light and swirling color, we disappeared into total darkness...

The screams of fury from the mysterious man still echoing inside my head.

CHAPTER 1

— • —

OLIVER - WELCOME TO HARRIET HIGH

I woke up in a cold sweat but kept my eyes shut so that I wouldn't be blinded by the fierce sunlight coming through the window. Rolling over, I clumsily fumbled for my phone on the wooden nightstand. My phone was vibrating like a chihuahua in the middle of the winter! Scratch paper, pencils, and pens rolled off and quietly thudded against the tan carpet below. Finally, I was able to grab a hold of my phone and swipe away the alarm. My phone went berserk every morning at six thirty so I wouldn't be late for school. If I was late for class one more time, I thought I'd be expelled.

I lifted my head and blinked at the dazzling sunlight that shimmered through the window. I got out of bed and walked into my giant closet that was the size of a highschool classroom. Clothes were strewn across the floor and a pile of shoes as tall as a mountain sat in the back left corner. Underwear was dangling off the ledge of my dresser that was pushed up against the right side of the closet. I picked out a crumpled pair of jeans, a green T-shirt that read: "CJ's Bowling Alley," and a pair of black socks. I took off my PJ's and put on my outfit, praying that they were clean. Right before I left, I looked at a mirror in the far corner of my room.

Wow...

I look good.

My brown hair was perfectly parted off to one side and there was not one zit on my face. I looked like Justin Timberlake with longer, darker hair... and a more pointed chin... and emerald green eyes...

You know what, forget what I said about the Justin Timberlake thing.

I bolted out of the room, jumped down the flight of stairs, and I walked into my favorite room of the house... the kitchen. The walls around me were a steel gray, and an island sat in the center of the room. My mom was leaning against the counter top, talking to one of her colleagues on the phone.

You see, my mom is a famous CEO for a company called, "T.G.I.F" or "Thank. God. It's. Froyo." They've created so many different froyos that are known throughout the world; flavors like Caramel Cream, Minty Tree, or Raz-Black Berry. My mom also has this way of lighting up the room even if she wasn't talking to you. She has a smile that makes her pearly white teeth shimmer even in the dark. She has tomato red hair and emerald eyes, just like mine.

"Morning, mom," I said, walking in and pulling open the fridge.

"Give me a moment, Francis... Hi, Oliver. Anything planned at school today?"

"Well one of our classes is making us go on a field trip and Rachel, Cyrus, and I were planning to go to the cafe after school. Then we were planning on going to..."

"That's nice dear." She turned away and continued talking to her colleague on the phone. I reached for my lunch bag and an apple, then closed the fridge door.

"Where's Dad?" I asked.

Mom turned to glare at me.

"He had to go to work early again. Now, I have someone on the phone, so I can't talk now, ok?"

"Ok." Even though my parents love me and everything, they never exactly had time for me. They were always either on the phone or running off to go to a meeting. but I don't mind at all. It's been like that ever since I can remember.

At seven, I closed the door to the garage and began to walk down our long driveway. The sun was peering through the trees that followed along the road, casting eerie shadows that crossed and turned like a big knot. When I turned and began walking down the sidewalk, I could still hear the man from my dream screaming in rage; just thinking about it made my hair stand on end. Honestly, that was the most terrifying dream I've ever had, and it felt so...

Real...

From behind me, I began to hear other students from my school laughing and talking, but only one voice stuck out from the crowd that made me smile.

"Hey, Oliver!" Fin, a senior like me in highschool, ran up and fist bumped me. He had dark, curly black hair and silver eyes. He wore a football jersey and navy blue jeans.

"What's up?" I asked.

"Well... Today I'm trying out for the football team!"

"Yeah I can tell," I said, looking at his football jersey before rolling my eyes. "You always try out for the football team, and you always get quarterback."

"Well who knows! Maybe someone might beat me in tryouts!" Fin said. He's always thinking about his version of the bright side.

"Are you trying out for any sports?" he asked.

"Nah," I said, shaking my head. "There's no way I could without falling on my face!"

"You've never tried," he trilled. He looked over his shoulder as a few girls smiled at him. He winked as he smiled back at them, and I heard the girls burst into a crazy fit of giggles.

"Oh yeah?" I said, drawing his attention back to me. "What about that time in fifth grade when I fell into a puddle of mud on the soccer field? I made a fool of myself in front of the entire class!" Fin laughed and patted me on the back. The sun seemed to wink in laughter, too, as it shimmered through the trees around us.

"Just because you tripped on Maya's flailing shoelaces as you tried to take the ball from her doesn't mean you shouldn't try again." I made a sound like an angry bull and shrugged my shoulders. We walked down the road and talked about our weekend. Apparently, Fin and his parents had attended three different parties for his father's new promotion.

By now I think you guys probably know what kind of people my friends and I are...

We are the rich kids. Well... Sure we are the kids of rich people, but it's not like we wanted to be rich! If we had our choice, we would want to be like everyone else who had parents with normal jobs.

When we finally turned the corner, we walked down a paved drive to a large, glass paned school that reflected the sun's rays. The grass was cut perfectly even, and there were no weeds in sight. Bushes lined the edge of the school's property like a vast wall. A marble sign read, "Harriet High school - A high school full of possibilities!" Harriet High school is known for MIH, or Most Intelligent Homosapiens, meaning that this school is a place where you better work hard and have good grades. However, if you have more money than normal people they cancel that smart factor out, which isn't exactly a good thing. Most of the boys here have the brain capacity of a blubber fish. They mainly like to push each other around and grunt. The girls... they'd rather gossip and mess with each others' hair than do their homework, which is what they do a lot of the time. But some kids, like Fin and I, do care about our grades and our future after high school.

Don't worry, you'll meet the others that are like us, too.

We entered the front door to a vast area that was bustling with students. Girls were laughing and taking selfies with each other; boys were throwing footballs back and forth, and teachers stood outside their doors, welcoming students into their classrooms and ignoring the chaos around them. Fin and I parted ways as he began to walk to his AP Geometry class and I walked to my extra curricular Cognitive Psychology class. I entered the classroom, and a girl waved her hand at me, smiling. I waved back and sat down next to her, my chair creaking.

"Hi, Oliver!"

"Hey, Racheal."

"How was your weekend?"

"It was good," I answered. "What about yours?"

"It was great!" Racheal said, ecstatically. "I started testing my new chemical compound. So far, it's been working great! It seems that instead of curing the mice of the disease I gave them, it actually gives them the ability to pick each other up!" All of this she said so fast that my brain began to hurt. Racheal is the smartest kid in the school. You could try to train your dog to sit by giving them treats, but Racheal can give your dog a chemical compound in their water and make them do flips and jump from building to building like a superhero. She doesn't know how she does it, but everyone agrees that it's one of the most intriguing things about her. But that's not the only thing people say is intriguing about her. She's also, brace yourself...

Goth.

I know right? You weren't exactly expecting that, huh? Her idol is this crazy female scientist that was goth and solved crimes in a TV show she watched. Racheal's goal is to become a forensic scientist that goes around solving crimes, and she one day hopes to win the Nobel Peace Prize. I think it's a long shot, but, hey, Rachael is Rachael.

Racheal has black hair with a lime green streak on the right side. Her hair is always tied up in pigtails that flow down on the sides of her head. She also wears spiked bracelets on both wrists as well as a choker, and her eyes are the color of caramel. Today she was wearing black torn jeans, a lime green shirt with a white skull in the center, and tall black boots with golden zippers on the side.

"Alright, class, let's get started," our teacher, Mrs. Leasel, said, clapping her hands together. Everyone fell silent and focused their attention on her. "Today we are going to study the brain. Now, the brain can differ from one organism to another. Some are small, and some are large. That is why today we are studying the human brain and its neurons and hormones that send signals to the body to react to certain circumstances throughout a persons' life." She clapped her hands together, and the lights went out. Then, her electric smart board turned on, and a diagram of the human body materialized on the screen. She tapped her screen, and the diagram zoomed in on the brain.

"Now, who can tell me an estimation of how many neurons the brain has?" Mrs. Leasel asked the class. Rachael's hand shot into the air like a cannonball, missing my face by an inch. Mrs. Leasel saw and pointed to Rachael.

"There are around eighty-six *billion* neurons in the human brain," Racheal answered.

"Correct!" Mrs. Leasel said, smiling. "Now, with that many neurons, our reactions to situations are quicker. For example: Who can tell me how many earthquakes there have been over the past two weeks?"

"About twenty-seven earthquakes," a kid to my left said. "That's almost twice a day."

"Indeed, there have been twenty-seven earthquakes over the past couple of weeks. However, I'm guessing that none of you just stood there like statues and did nothing, right?"

"We went under tables so nothing could fall on our heads," I responded, raising my hand in the air.

"Now that," Mrs. Leasel said, "is a reaction that your neurons cause when a situation like that happens. You were told to always duck and cover so you could protect your head. Your reaction of getting under the table was caused by neurons in your brain sending messages to your body to take cover..." For the next fifty minutes, we continued to learn how neurons and hormones affect people's reactions and how habits are formed to create certain decisions in specific environments. Finally, the bell rang and we packed up our things.

"Don't forget to study for your test that's next Thursday on perception, learning, attention, categorization, and problem solving for humans!"

"Well, that wasn't as interesting as usual." Racheal said, frowning. "I've never seen Mrs. Leasel so..."

"Uninterested in a topic about science?" I said.

"Yeah. She always does games and fun online challenges to help us learn about the topic. All she was doing today was stating facts and asking questions. It's like a flame has gone out inside her head."

"Yeah..." I trailed off. Suddenly, I heard someone scream, and I turned around to see whom it came from.

"Did you hear that?" I asked.

"What?" Racheal turned around to face me.

"That scream. It came from right behind us."

"Oliver, nobody screamed. Stop messing with me, bro!" She punched me in the shoulder, but I didn't react. I continued to look around to find who screamed.

"I swear someone screamed behind us..."

"Oliver?" I turned to look at Racheal. Her expression looked a little worried. "Are you feeling alright? Maybe you should go to the office! Perhaps you have a fever or..."

"No, I'm fine," I said, putting a hand on her shoulder. "Let's just go."

CHAPTER 2

— ❧ —

OLIVER - THE TRIP

We parted ways as she went to her Phy. Ed. class and I went to CAP English Honors class. When I entered, I looked around to see everyone standing up with their backpacks over their shoulders. Some of them were holding lunch boxes in their hands while others were on their phones texting people in other classes. I saw Fin and two other friends of ours standing next to each other in the corner of the room. All of them were talking happily, and when I walked over, one of them hugged me.

"Bonjour, Oliver!"

"Hey, Harper."

"Sup, Oliver."

Harper let go of me, and I turned to see Cyrus looking at me.

"Cyrus, what's up, man?"

"Nothing much. You?"

"I'm doing well," I said, smiling.

Cyrus and Harper are two of the most popular kids in the school. Cyrus always wears soccer jerseys and bright orange shoes with white socks. He has sandy brown hair, brown eyes with brown flecks around the pupils, and freckles covering his cheeks. With all of that put together, he looks so much younger than he really is. He's a year older than Fin, Racheal, and I because he was held back a year for going too fast on his tests. Harper is a completely different story. She's two years younger than us but is so smart that she was able to skip two years. However, you shouldn't let that fool you into thinking that she's a nerd. Harper has blue, silver eyes and honey blond hair that always glows in the light. Today, she wore a white crop-top, blue denim jeans, and clean, white shoes with a black lightning bolt symbol stretched across the right side.

"Are you ready for the class trip?" Harper asked, excitingly. "I hear we're going to the new museum that just opened a few months ago!"

"Yeah," I said. "The way my father talks about it, he makes it sound like it's going to be the biggest tourist attraction in America by the end of this year."

"I wouldn't be surprised if it is. It's been all over the place. On the news, in magazines, newspapers, even on billboards outside of Crystal Falls!"

"Why are we even going to it anyway?" Fin asked. "It's just a museum." Then, his face lit up as a thought came to him. "We should go to an amusement park!"

"Because," Harper said, "we are learning about myths and legends for our current unit, silly! Don't you ever listen to the teacher?"

"I do!" Fin said, offended. Then he muttered, "It just never sinks in." We laughed at his remark but fell silent as our teacher, Ms. Hart, entered the room.

"The buses are outside the main entrance. Please walk in a line, and, since there are other classes going on, *please stay quiet!*"

We all nodded, showing that we understood. Then, we walked out of the classroom and out of the school.

Riding on the bus isn't exactly fun when you're in high school. A lot of students think that they can get away with things like smoking, throwing footballs back and forth, and making rude gestures to each other that would make your grandma have a heart attack! However, Harper, Fin, Cyrus, and I always sat in the front two rows and talked about college. You see, we all have different ideas about where we are going to go, but we still plan to go to colleges in the same state. We don't want to worry about not seeing each other during the school year. Harper's planning to go to a fashion design school. Fin is planning on going to a college to be a math professor. Racheal is going to go to a science college that mainly focuses on crime investigations and cold cases, and Cyrus is planning on going to a college for sports to try to become the next Hall of Fame soccer player.

"So, Oliver," said Racheal, looking at me from the other side of the bus, "have you decided about where you are going to go to college?"

13

"No," I said, looking a little abashed. For the past three years, I had been trying to figure out which college I would be going to that's close to my friends, but when my parents found out about what my friends and I were planning, they told me that I have to become the next CEO of Thank. God. It's. Froyo. But it's not what I want! I want to be able to travel around the world, exploring new places and learning about other cultures and their traditions. So, I secretly signed up for as many colleges that focus on geography and travel as I could that were in the local area. Only two accepted my request: Border State University and Rockefeller College.

"You know," Fin said, "one way or another, you're going to have to tell your parents what you did with your application."

"I know that," I said, looking away, "but you know what they'd do! They'd take the application, force me to go to a college that focuses on business, and ground me for the rest of my life!"

"Oh, Oliver! You know they would never do such a thing!" Harper leaned over from the other side of the seat and patted my thigh.

"Thanks..." I said. I put my hand on her hand and smiled. We then changed the subject and began to play Rock, Paper, Scissors for another ten minutes.

With a loud thud, making the entire bus quake as we hit the curb, we turned into the long entrance of the museum. On both sides of the bus, all you could see was the green blur of tall bushes that lined the road. The road ahead of us was newly paved and covered in black tar that made it look as if we were floating inches above a bottomless pit. After a couple more minutes, a large castle that was the size of about four football fields came into view as we neared the parking lot of the museum. The castle walls were made of dark, gray stone with green, flower covered vines that seemed to glow in the morning light. Windows glinted like sparkling glitter, and a large fountain in the center of the entrance way gushed out water, making graceful arcs in the air.

When the bus stopped at the entrance, we all stood up and filed out. I took a deep breath, taking in the sweet smell of flowers and freshly cut grass.

"Isn't this great?" Racheal asked.

"I've never seen anything like it," Harper said, in awe.

"Yeah. Remember when this place was just a pile of ruins?" I asked.

"Oh yeah! It looked like a mountain from far away."

"Class," Ms. Hart called out, "we are going inside. So, please stay quiet! Last time, you guys were on a field trip similar to this one, you sounded like a bunch of hooligans!"

A couple of kids snickered at the remark, mainly because they were the people who were the hooligans. As we walked through the doors, we all looked up. Some girls ooed and awed at the polished ebony wood that had golden paint snaking around it just like the vines outside. Green painted flowers were here and there along the ceiling. They were so realistic that I swear I could've reached up and plucked one off the ceiling. Our class took a right down a hallway, and an old man walked up to us. He was old and thin, maybe sixty or seventy. He also had wrinkles on his face that depicted how much he must smile, which was a lot, and his eyes were the color of chocolate, making me think of the chocolate cafe shop on Twenty-Second Street that my friends and I were planning on going to later that day. His hair was chalk white with a bald spot in the top center of his head, and he wore circular glasses that made his eyes look larger than normal, along with a navy-blue uniform that I could've sworn on my life was worth over a thousand dollars.

"Good morning!" The man said, his voice very high pitched. A few guys behind us snickered, and our teacher scowled at them before turning to look at the old man.

"Good morning!" Ms. Hart replied, smiling. "We are here for a school field trip."

"Ahhhhh, yes. I remember seeing your class on the tour schedule this morning. My name is Mr. Houdi, like Houdini without the 'ni' at the end," he chuckled. "Alright. Follow me." Our class began to walk behind him as he opened two huge, African blackwood doors with golden door knobs. It opened to a huge, open area that had a long, red carpet that led to the other side of the room. At the end of the red carpet, four golden raised thrones stood. Each throne was made the same size but had different carvings in the gold. Mr. Houdi suddenly stopped us in our tracks, making me bump into Harper accidentally.

"Sorry," I whispered.

"It's fine," she said, smiling.

"Now this," Mr. Houdi said, making the two of us go silent, "is the throne room of the royal family that lived here a long time ago. Now, their history has been shrouded in untold truth for the past five hundred years until very recently when an archeologist discovered an old diary of the youngest daughter of the last line of the family. Her name was Grace Williams. In the diary, she describes her family, her life in the castle, and her relationship with her older sister, Cora Williams, a girl who was supposedly destined to bring glory to her family and their home."

"What kind of glory?" Cyrus asked, raising his hand.

"I'm glad you asked. Mr..."

"Cyrus," he said. "Cyrus Miller."

"Well Mr. Miller, the kind of glory I'm talking about is a tradition of the royal family, a legend in fact, that prophesied the destruction of our world's greatest enemy."

"Can you tell us about it?" Fin asked. Some students around us groaned while everyone else nodded.

"Indeed I can!" Mr. Houdi said, smiling. We all huddled closer together so that we could listen to him. "The royal family believed that long ago, the world was created by a goddess that harnessed the sun's light. This goddess's name was Delphi. With one flick of her hand, she created the world we know today and allowed light to fill its dark emptiness. She gave life to animals and plants. She called the sun down to melt rocks and shape them into mountains. She even summoned the power of her divine spirit to give life to humans. But where there is light, there is always shadow..." Mr. Houdi paused to take a deep breath, then continued. As he spoke, the lights around us seemed to grow darker, and the air around us grew cold. "Malice... An entity that was created from everything that is negative: Fear, hate, despair, and death. This thing's primary goal is to destroy everything, and I mean everything, in its path. Malice has used many innocent lives in order to obtain this terrible glory. His only obstacle, however, was..." He gestured for us to follow him and we all walked quickly down the hallway, eager to hear more. We turned a corner and entered a room with a very large painting of a ten-year-old girl.

"Her," Mr. Houdi said, pointing at the girl.

"Who is that?" Asked a girl from the back of the group.

"That is Cora Williams." Mr. Houdi said. We all took a moment to admire her. In my opinion, Cora looked like a younger version of a girl from a Greek myth. Her hair was a lush brown, like a Rolo, her skin was a slight beige color, and her eyes were electric blue. She wore a long emerald, green dress with a golden belt as well as a golden crown that looked like a wreath around her head. I smiled a little as I realized that one of her front teeth was missing, and her crown was slightly tilted to the left side of her head.

"She looks so... princessy," the guy next to me said.

"That's because she *is* a princess, Christopher," Harper said, rolling her eyes. She and I glanced at each other and smiled.

Mr. Houdi continued, ignoring us. "Cora is a princess who is known for her young beauty. However, she is also known for her silence, as Cora's sister, Grace, has expressed in one entry of her diary. According to her, Cora acted like every little girl on the Earth until she was four when their mother was murdered. That was also the last time Grace ever recorded seeing Cora."

"Where did she go?" Cyrus asked, raising his hand.

"No one knows." Mr. Houdi said, shrugging. "Grace never wrote that down in her diary. Perhaps she may have never known." I stared in amazement. Someone must have been heartless in order to tear the two sisters apart. I looked over at my friends and saw that their faces looked shocked and sad, too.

Mr. Houdi talked for another five minutes about how each member of the royal family played a part in history, but I wasn't paying attention. In the back of my mind, I began to hear a voice; the same voice that was Cora? The girl from my dream? As our class began to walk down another hallway, the voice of Cora began to grow louder. She seemed to be yelling and grunting, as if she was fighting back something large. Then I heard my name, "Oliver."

I stopped and turned around quickly. Some students muttered under their breath as they moved around me. I looked left and right, but no one was behind me. Then I heard it again.

"Oliver... Help."

It was Cora's voice!

"Cora?" I whispered.

"Mr. Johnson," Ms. Hart called. "Is everything alright?"

I didn't answer.

"Oliver," Cora's voice echoed. "Help me... Please, there isn't much time. Go into the dungeon down the hall and to the left."

"Mr. Johnson, stop messing around and- Wait! Call for security!" But it was too late. Before Mr. Houdi could pull out his walkie-talkie, I had already bolted back down the hallway, turned left, and hopped over a sign that read: "Dungeon! Authorized Personnel ONLY!"

"They are coming," Cora's voice whispered. "Hide." I hid behind a curtain as I heard multiple security guards run past. When I thought the coast was clear, I ran down a stairwell. The entire dungeon smelled of mildew and was made of stone with rusty metal jail bars that lined either side.

"Good. Now, tap the center tile. That will open a secret passage. Hurry! We are running out of time!"

I ran to the center of the dungeon and tapped the tile with my hand. Immediately, a warm feeling began to spread as a mysterious power pulsed through my body. The tile glowed golden and about 10 feet away, a tile disappeared as a ladder formed on one side of the hole. Cautiously, and curiously, I climbed down and ended up in a large, vast cave. It was the size of fourteen football fields with stalactites hanging from the ceiling like giant swords. It was very dark, the only light was from the dungeon about 100 feet above my head. When I squinted to the center of the cave, however, I could see a slight gold and magenta glow that kept flashing. I started to walk towards the light when I suddenly tripped over a pile of goo. When my body came in contact with it, the goo immediately began to wrap around me. I screamed in terror as I felt my flesh being eaten away. I yanked my arm out of it, and my skin regrew instantly.

"What the heck is that stuff!?!" I yelled, my voice making me sound like I was a soprano.

"That is black matter," Cora's voice said. That was when I suddenly realized that her voice sounded weak, like she was getting tired. "Whatever you do, don't touch it again."

I began to walk more cautiously just in case there was more of that goo around. When I was about 20 feet from the glowing light, I could see a large chasm that dropped into a pit where the light came from.

"Now Oliver," Cora said. "I need you to-" I heard Cora gasp and suddenly...

Everything went quiet.

"Cora?" I called out.

Silence. Then a loud roar tore through the air, the same roar from my dreams. The earth began to quake like it never had before. I heard a cracking noise and looked down to see that the rock beneath my feet had long, deep cuts in it. I tried to take a step back, but before I could, the floor dropped. My head collided with a piece of rock, and I fell into an endless pit of darkness as the ceiling caved in on itself.

CHAPTER 3

CORA - I AM CORA

All I remembered was darkness. Darkness that covered my eyes like a blanket, blocking out the sun. Then a flash of light and the world around me turned white. I could hear beeping and worried voices. The smell of lemon and chemicals filled my nostrils. When I opened my eyes I saw a world I've never seen before...

And I was in it.

There were these weird blocks that had lights and zig zags moving across them. I could hear someone saying, "She's awake! The girl! Over here!" My body hurt so badly that when I tried to lift my arm, a stabbing pain went through me. Someone walked over and looked down at me. It was a man. He had gray hair and gray, sunken eyes. He was wearing a white, long jacket and a teal colored mask.

"Hello. I'm glad you're awake."

"Wha... Where am I?" I asked. "Who are you?"

"I'm Doctor Johnson. You're in the hospital."

"Hospital?"

"Have you ever been in a hospital before?"

I paused trying to remember. Everything before now seemed to be gone. All I could remember were flashing magenta and gold lights.

"No, I don't think so."

"Really?" His voice sounded curious, as if he's never heard someone say that.

"Well then, let's start off with your name."

I paused, trying to think. *Why couldn't I remember anything?*

"I don't... have one?"

He looked at me, his face full of shock. Then he wrote something down on his sheet of paper and looked at me again. "You seem to be suffering from some sort of amnesia," said Doctor Johnson. "Rest assured it can be treated, but we need to find out what type of amnesia it is. For now, you'll stay here with the other patient."

I stared at him, confused. "Other patient?"

"Yes. The boy that was with you. His name is Oliver Johnson," he paused. "My grandson, in fact."

"Oh?" *Why did my brain have to be so foggy and mushy?* I turned my head to the left and saw a boy, my age, sleeping in a bed. He had brown hair, like mine, and had a huge cloth on one side of his forehead and the sleeves of his shirt were torn. Small treads were weaved into some sections of his head and arms.

"Miss?" I looked back at Doctor Johnson. "Do you have any idea why my grandson was with you or how you ended up at the bottom of a chasm?"

"I'm sorry, no. I didn't even know who he was until now."

"I see," he said, frowning. "Well until both of you recover, you will stay here. The reporters are going crazy outside the room, trying to take pictures of you two. I'll be back later today, and nurses will come to see if there is anything you need."

"Ok."

Doctor Johnson then turned around and left, closing the door behind him. I continued to try and move around, even though, I must admit, it hurt a lot. I was able to turn my head and lift my arms without it hurting too much. I actually screamed in shock when I saw something stuck out of the back of my hand, like a tube. That's when the first nurse came in. She had black hair that was tied in a bun, and she wore a teal mask as well.

"Are you alright dear?"

"What is this thing in my hand!?!"

"It's an IV dear. Calm down. Take a deep breath."

I took a deep breath and closed my eyes, trying to slow down my pounding heart.

"So what does this... IV do?" I asked, trying to sound calm.

"It keeps water in your body so you don't die of dehydration."

"Oh. Ok," I said, skeptically.

Silence.

"Do you need anything else dear?" the nurse asked.

"No, thank you."

"Ok, I'll be here if you need me."

She left, and I lay there silently for the rest of the day. Doctor Johnson came in every now and then, checking on me and Oliver. For the entire time, the boy lay there unconscious, drooling. It was night before Oliver's eyes fluttered open. For a moment, he moaned and looked around. When he saw me, he blinked in shock.

"Who are you?" he asked.

"Honestly, I don't know," I said. "Your name is Oliver, right?"

"Yes," he said, perplexed. "How did you know?"

"Our doctor told me who you are. He's your grandfather."

"Oh yeah. Grandpa John," Oliver said, sitting up and rubbing his head.

"Well at least you remember who you are and who he is. I don't remember anything."

Oliver furrowed his eyebrows in confusion. "How come?"

"I don't know!" I tried sitting up but gasped as a stabbing pain went through my chest; I laid back down

"You ok?"

"No." Then a thought came to me as I lay there. "How did you end up near me?" I asked. "You and I were found at the bottom of a chasm, and no one can explain how."

It was as if I could hear Oliver's mind whirling, like he didn't want to admit something shameful. Then he flicked on a switch near us, and a light above our heads turned on. He smiled, and I could see that his cheeks were slightly pink, as if he was embarrassed.

"Well, I have a theory about why we were together," Oliver said, a little awkward. "I had a dream. About a girl that looks just like you. We were running away from a person called Malice. Later that afternoon, our class went on a field trip to a museum of an old castle. We learned about a girl who was alive over five hundred years ago and she looked just like you, too. Then later, I heard a voice telling me to head into the castle dungeon. That's when I got separated from the class and ended up near an abandoned area of the castle. Then there was another earthquake, and the floor collapsed beneath me. I remember my head hitting a piece of rock, but that's it." He said all of that so fast, as if the quicker he got it off his chest, the better. I lay there silent for a while, trying to understand what he was saying.

"Wait," Oliver said, his face breaking into realization. "What if that girl I saw in my dream and in the museum was really you?"

"But wouldn't I have remembered it?" I said, looking at him.

"Well if you lost your memory, perhaps it means that you hit your head or something."

"I mean, I guess that could be the case... But the doctors said that my head was fine. Nothing was wrong with it."

"Hmmm... Well then I don't know," he said, trailing off. We sat there in silence again until finally, my eyes began to droop. Oliver must have seen it because he smiled at me.

"You can go to sleep. I'm just going to stay awake for a little longer." I nodded and closed my eyes, immediately falling into a blissful sleep.

For the following days, Oliver and I stayed in the hospital. People, called news reporters and camera men, cast shadows across our curtained windows and doors as their cameras flashed hazy white lights. At least, that's what Oliver explained to me.

"Why do they want to come into our room?" I asked as Doctor Johnson switched out my IV bag.

"Well, ever since you and Oliver were found, everyone in Crystal Falls has been craving more information about how you and Oliver got down in the chasm. They also want to know who you are."

"So, I'm guessing you still don't know exactly who I am then?" I asked, my heart sinking.

"Sadly, no. We've interviewed several people in the city asking if they know who you are, but no one has recognized you." He looked at me and saw my face, and his expression turned sympathetic. He patted me on the shoulder. "Don't worry. We are doing everything we can. Soon, we'll be able to figure it out." Within a couple minutes of checking Oliver's arm and head, he left, closing the door behind him. I put my pillow over my head and groaned.

"Hey," Oliver said, his voice muffled by the pillow. "My grandpa will do everything he can to help. He's great at keeping his word."

I ignored him and stayed silent. *If I was from this area, wouldn't someone have come and gotten me by now? I mean... That's what I would've done if I found out that my child was in the hospital and didn't remember anything.* But... Then something that Oliver said to me from a few days ago whispered in my head like a soft breeze... *"I had a dream. About a girl that looks just like you... Later that afternoon, our class went on a field trip to a museum of an old castle. We learned about a girl who was alive over five hundred years ago and she looked just like you, too. What if that girl I saw in my dream and in the museum was really you..!"* My heart began to pound vigorously. *What if he was right? What if I am the girl from his dream?* I shivered at the thought. *Why am I so old?*

After a few minutes, I took the pillow off of my head and glanced at Oliver to see him sitting up in his bed watching me.

"What?" I groaned, looking up at the ceiling.

"You don't believe me, do you?" He said, frowning.

29

"Well... no I don't," I said. Oliver didn't say anything. I sat up and turned to face him.

"But what if... what if you're right about me being the girl you saw in your dream and at that museum?" Silence once more; it wasn't our normal silence. Instead, it was tense, like a rubber band being pulled tight. Oliver opened his mouth. Then closed it, as if he was trying to decide what to say.

"Then I guess your name would be Cora." Oliver said.

I thought about that for a while. *Cora. I like that name.* "Alright. I guess I'll call myself Cora. At least until I remember what my real name is." I smiled at him and he smiled at me. A weird feeling went through my body like an electric shock.

How strange...

❧❧❧❧❧ ❦❦❦❦❦

Finally, after two weeks of being in the hospital, Doctor Johnson gave Oliver and I a "clean bill of health". Apparently, that's a good thing. I am still sticking with the name Cora. Everyone thinks the name suits me really well, as if I was born to be called Cora.

"So, does that mean that we get to leave?" I asked Doctor Johnson. He nodded.

"My parents are coming to pick me up from the hospital this afternoon," Oliver said, getting up from the hospital bed. "Maybe my parents would let you come with and.."

"Oliver, she's not allowed to come with you to your home," Doctor Johnson interrupted. "Not unless your family are foster parents, and I know that they aren't. She will be staying here until we find out who she is." Oliver looked at me, and I could sense how he felt: disappointed. Honestly, I kind of felt the same way. Over the past couple of weeks, we'd grown close. He'd taught me a lot that I've forgotten, and he always made me laugh.

That afternoon, Oliver's mother and father came to pick him up. His father, Mr. Johnson, was on the phone for the entire time, but he did pat Oliver's shoulder for a second. Before they left, Oliver hugged me and took my hand, smiling.

"Don't worry," Oliver said. "I'll see if my parents can pull some strings to let you come stay with us. They can do that kind of stuff." I nodded and hugged him again.

"Thank you, Oliver."

The moment he left, I wished that I would've hugged him tighter than what I had that day because an unpleasant feeling began to spread through me, telling me that things would not be the same the next time we'd see each other.

CHAPTER 4

— • —

OLIVER - I WISH I WOULD'VE KNOWN WHAT WOULD HAPPEN NEXT

On the drive back to our house, Mom and Dad were on their phones, talking to clients and employees. They hadn't said one word to me so far, which is not unusual for them. I kept thinking about Cora or whatever her real name was. She looks identical to the girl I saw in my dream. Brown hair, pale beige color skin, and electric blue eyes with golden specks flecked inside her irises. She was so beautiful...

WOAH WOAH WAIT WHAT!?!? Did I just think that? Did I just think she was... beautiful? I felt my stomach begin to churn like batter in a mixer. *Why would I ever think that? I never liked anyone. Ever. There is no way that now I would. Would I?*

We arrived at our house at about four in the afternoon. My dad finally got off the phone to tell us that he had to go back to work, and my mom ran to her office downstairs the moment we went inside. That left me by myself in the empty silence of the rest of our house. I went upstairs and opened my bedroom door and sat down on my bed. My pencils, pens, and paper that were once scattered on the ground had been neatly placed back onto my nightstand and my bed had been made. One of the maids must have cleaned up my room. That's when I got a notification on my phone. It was the group chat that my friends and I made a few years ago. The text was from Harper.

(Harper): "OMG! Oliver r u back home? I just saw ur car drive past our house! We've been worried sick! Plz respond ASAP!"

I smiled at the text and sent my reply. Within seconds, Racheal, Harper, and Cyrus saw and responded to it.

(Racheal): "YAAAAAAY!!!! That's fantastic! The hospital wouldn't let us enter ur ward because of the news reporters blocking the entrance. They said they didn't want to risk bad press! It was so frustrating!"

(Cyrus): "Yeah, it was pretty upsetting. They didn't even tell us if u were alive! We were betting that u were, but it was still ridiculous that they wouldn't tell us anything."

(Racheal): "Don't be silly Cyrus. Of course they told us that he was alive."

No one responded after that. I decided that since I knew it was the end of the school day, I might as well ask them if they wanted to come over.

(Oliver): "Hey, do u guys wanna come over and hangout?"

The three profile pictures teleported next to my text to show that Racheal, Cyrus, and Harper saw it.

(Cyrus): "Sure I'm down. I'll be over in 5."

(Racheal): "Same here! SYS!"

(Harper): "On my way!"

My heart leapt with joy. I get to see my friends after weeks of being in the hospital. I'd get to see Racheal, Cyrus, and Harper, maybe even Cora. Wait a minute... I had to slap myself in order to snap myself out of the thought. Cora's still in the hospital. She isn't coming over.

What is wrong with me?

I went back downstairs and paced the kitchen until there was a loud knock on the door. I rushed over to the front entrance and whipped the door open. In a flash of color, Harper bolted through the door, wrapped her arms around me, and hugged me tightly as she burst into tears.

"Wow. Harper, I know that I've been gone for a few weeks, but I haven't been gone that long."

"I know," she said, letting go and wiping her eyes. "But I'm just so glad to see you."

"Mind if we join the welcome home party?" came Rachel's voice. Harper and I turned to see Racheal and Cyrus waiting at the front door. Racheal wore a black tank top and skirt that just touched her knees as well as a pair of black converse hightops. Her hair was down so that it went past her elbows. Harper pushed me away and looked down at her feet. *Was it just me or were her cheeks turning bright pink?* I ignored the thought and smiled at Rachel.

"Of course! Come on in." They walked in, and we all sat down in the living room. Racheal and Harper sat down on the beige colored couch while Cyrus and I sat in the white leather chairs in the corner of the room.

"Wait, where's Fin?" I asked, looking around.

"I think Fin's still working his shift at the restaurant, but he should've been done by now."

"Maybe he's working late," Rachel said, shrugging.

"Probably," Harper said. Then, she turned to focus on me. "So, tell us Oliver, what happened? Why did you run off at the museum, and why is the news talking about a girl being with you in the hospital?" She said all of this so fast that it took a moment for me to comprehend the questions she had just asked. I took a deep breath and explained everything about Cora's voice talking to me, the cave, the weird light, and waking up in the hospital. When I finished, my friends were staring at me in disbelief.

"So, let me get this straight," Cyrus said, leaning forward in his chair. "The girl we were learning about at the museum was the girl you were with at the hospital?"

"Yes, at least that's what I believe," I said, nodding.

"And she doesn't remember anything? Nothing at all?"

"That's right."

"Maybe she hit her head like you did," Racheal noted. "If she had head trauma, it could be the reason why she lost her memory."

"That's what I thought at first," I said, shaking my head. "But, they checked for head injuries, and she didn't have any. In fact, she only had a few cuts. Even a broken rib they x-rayed had already almost healed."

"That's weird," Cyrus said, smiling slyly, one eyebrow raised. "But anyway, what did you think of her? Was she perfect? She looks like she'd be your type..."

I opened my mouth, about to spill my momentary feelings I had in the car on the way home from the hospital, but I stopped. There was no way I was going to tell them about that. That would be completely embarrassing.

"Dude, that's gross. A girl I just met? No way!" I lied. Cyrus laughed. Harper was glancing at me as if hurt by something, but I looked away.

"So, is she still at the hospital?" Racheal said, purposefully changing the subject.

"Yes," I answered.

"But haven't her parents picked her up yet?" Cyrus asked. "Surely, they would have heard about her by now from the news?"

"That's the thing though," I said. "If she really is who we're thinking, her parents are dead right?"

"Yes, but who's to say that's the case?" Racheal argued. "That girl would then be over five hundred years old!"

The doorbell rang and Harper jumped up, sprinting out of the room. A moment later, Fin came in wearing his restaurant uniform with Harper following behind. "Sorry that I'm late guys," he said, taking off his sports hat. "Billy, our old manager, had an announcement to make about his retirement. He said that his position was going to be open, but I'm glad you're back, Oliver. I saw the text messages and came as quickly as I could."

"Thanks, Fin. We were just talking about-"

"That girl on the news with you?" Fin asked, interrupting me. "I was guessing that. So, what did you think of her?"

"Oh my gosh, seriously? You, too?" I said, rolling my eyes. Fin smirked and sat down on the white fluffy carpet.

༄༄༄༄ ༺༺༺༺

For the next few days, we hung out and talked back and forth about what I missed at school as if it was just an ordinary week. That's what I like about my friends. They just want everything to be normal like I do.

But that's when my whole world turned upside down. Suddenly, our phones went berserk and began to wail like police sirens. We all whipped them out and saw something that made my heart stop. A little white square with a red triangle popped up on my screen which read:

CHILD ABDUCTION!

(AMBER ALERT)

Unknown Name

CF MAR1P0SA

Black Chevy Equinox

Last seen - Crystal Falls Hospital

"Wait, turn on the news!" Rachel said. I lunged for the remote on the coffee table and turned on the news channel. A tall brunette new reporter, wearing a long pink dress was in the parking lot of the hospital Cora was in. To her left, there was a huge crowd of news reporters being barricaded off by a swat team and police officers. In the background, I saw firefighters and another group of police officers wearing hazmat suits. I could see that they were carrying out bodies... but they looked as if they were already almost bone. *How was that possible?*

"That's right, folks," the news reporter said. "Just moments ago, the police received an urgent 9-1-1 call about a suspicious man coming into the hospital, muttering about something before the call was abruptly ended by a high pitched scream. By the time police had arrived, a massacre had occurred, and everyone in the hospital was killed. The only people reported alive are the man and a girl that a witness saw. The girl matched the description of the patient discovered in the earthquake at the museum. The witness claims that she was bound in black chains and was shoved in a black Chevy that drove west. The entire town is on the verge of panic, and if anyone has any more information on the girl, please contact-" Before she could finish, I turned off the TV and walked out of the room.

"Oliver, where are you going? Oliver!"

But it was too late. I grabbed my coat and keys as I ran out the door.

Chapter 5

Cora - If I Could Turn Back the Clock

Honestly, I would've gone with Oliver and his family to his house in a heartbeat. There, I said it. Although, I probably would have gone with anyone if I would've known what would have happened next.

After Oliver and his parents left, Doctor Johnson closed the door and looked at me, his expression sympathetic. "Don't worry, Cora. I assure you that as soon as we find your parents, you'll get to go home, too. Then, maybe your parents can tell us your real name."

"Yeah…" I said, getting back into my hospital bed and shoving my face into the pillow. "If we find them."

The next week was rough. People kept trying to force their way into my room. There was even a guy who came in wanting to meet me. He even threatened to shoot people, so in the end, the entire hospital went into something called "lockdown". When doctors and nurses tried to check in on me, a rush of news reporters would desperately try to get in. They'd scream over each other, asking me questions, but I didn't answer any of them. Most of their questions I didn't even know how to answer, having lost my memory and all.

Even through all of that, two things kept me up at night. One, I felt that I was missing something. Two, everytime I thought about Oliver, my whole body seemed to grow numb, and my heart soared like the hawk that flies past my window every afternoon. I've tried explaining it to Doctor Johnson and the other workers there, but my throat seemed to close in on itself as if it didn't want to work. That made me even more nervous because maybe it meant that I really was sick. I mean, I don't think that that's the case but still, I don't think it's normal.

One day, at least ten nurses and doctors entered, smiling at me like they had just won the lottery.

"Great news!" sang one of the nurses. "Your father is here to pick you up! He heard about you on the news and is so glad that you're safe."

"What?" I said, astonished.

"Yeah! Isn't it great!?!" another nurse said, her voice sounding unnaturally shrill. When I looked closer, I noticed her eyes looked glossy and distant; trancelike. In fact, all of their eyes looked glossy and distant. That's when the hair on the back of my neck began to prickle.

"W-where is he?" I asked, trying to stay calm.

"He's on the first floor in the main lobby, dear. We'll take you to him if you'd like."

"But doesn't Doctor Johnson need to..." But within seconds the nurses and doctors picked me up, put me in a wheelchair, I think that's what it's called, and pushed me out of the room. The light in the hallway was flickering, making the place seem really creepy and haunted. Even when I took a breath in, my lungs seemed to be filled with unbreathable air. That's when we turned the corner, and I gasped, spluttering in terror.

The entire hallway was filled with bodies. Some were plastered to the ceiling or walls, others were laying limply on the ground. A magenta black goo seemed to be slowly encasing the corpses. I could see it eating away at their flesh and disintegrating the bone. I immediately recognized one of the bodies as Doctor Johnson himself, half of his body missing under a pile of goo. I screamed in terror, but one of the nurses covered my mouth with a scented cloth. Instantly, my mind went numb, and I passed out cold in the wheelchair.

$$\text{❦❦❦❦❦} \quad \text{❦❦❦❦❦}$$

I woke up to a dazzling light. When my eyes re-focused, the light seemed to be coming from a lamp directly above my head. I tried to move but my hands came in contact with something that looked like black chains. Pain shot through my body like electricity. I yelped, and a soft laugh echoed around me, making goosebumps rise on my shoulders.

"In all of my years, I've never imagined seeing you again, Cora," a voice hissed from the darkness.

"Let me go!" I yelled into the darkness.

"I don't think so..." *Was it just me or did everytime the voice talked, a quiet 'hiss' seemed to follow after it.* I squinted, trying to see where the voice was coming from.

"Who are you?" I asked. "Show yourself!" Silence. Then, to my right, a figure moved out of the shadows and into the light.

My brain couldn't even comprehend what I was looking at. The top of the man looked almost normal. He had short, buzz cut hair, a scrunched up nose, pale skin, and yellow eyes with slit pupils like a snake's. However, his legs seemed to melt together to form a scaly serpent's tail that was as long as a hospital bed. The "man" wore obsidian armor on his chest that seemed to glow a faint magenta. When he smiled at me, I could see two blood stained fangs and a forked tongue that flickered between his lips.

"What the..."

"Now don't be rude, Cora. It's not nice to be disrespectful to an old friend." The man-creature thing pouted. I stared at him, confused.

"What?"

"Come on. Surely, you remember me? I was your family's royal advisor! We were practically friends!" I tried to remember, but I couldn't. *What is this guy talking about?*

"I don't believe this," he said, almost sounding hurt. "My old friend doesn't even remember who I am... Well that's unfortunate." His tongue flickered as he looked at me up and down, taking it all in. In the back of my mind, I knew that I couldn't trust this guy, but I don't know why I was thinking that. I mean he did just say that he was my old friend. So I should trust him...

Right?

"Well," the thing said. "There *must* be something that I can do to help... I know!" He slithered back a few paces and held his left hand up. A purple fire erupted from his palm and hovered just above his fingertips.

"Uh," I stammered. "What are you-" He shot the fire straight at me, and I was engulfed in flame. The moment the fire hit my body, flashes of memories raced through my mind. I saw a younger version of myself, cradling my baby sister in my arms. Then, I saw myself looking up into my mother's face as her hand stroked my hair while she sang me a lullaby. After that, I saw the castle falling apart as power flowed through my veins and I tackled the shadowy figure of Malice deep into the dungeon ruins. But then I remembered who Deku really was, and when the memories finally came to a stop, I could feel rage boiling inside me like hot water in a pot.

"I remember. I remember it all," I said as a familiar power began to slowly spread through my body like wildfire. "And we are *not* friends!" Deku's pupils turned to slits as he sneered.

"Then I'm guessing you know why you're here?"

"Yes I do, but it won't work." I said, looking around. Surely someone would realize that I was missing from the hospital.

"What do you mean?" Deku snapped as he slithered closer until he was nearly an inch from my face. His forked tongue tickled my nose, but I ignored it.

"I don't know where it is," I said coolly.

"LIAR!" Within seconds, his tail whipped out from behind him and hit my face. It sliced through my skin, and I felt blood begin to dribble down my cheek. I tried my best to not cry from the stinging, but it hurt... A lot.

"It's true!" I yelled at Deku. I heard my voice crack, and I cleared my throat. Deku began to slither back and forth in front of me, as if pacing. "My family never told me where it was! Only my parents and Luke knew the location of the staff!"

"DO NOT LIE TO ME, CORA! I KNOW PERFECTLY WELL THAT YOU KNOW WHERE IT IS!" He screamed

"But I don't, Deku. Can't you see? So, why don't you just let me go and..."

"You really think I'm going to fall for that? How pathetic," he spat in my face and pulled something out from behind him. It was a huge staff that was made of the same material as his armor because it, too, glowed a faint magenta. It was taller than him and had a crescent moon shaped spear head that was molted at the top.

"As you can see your good friend, my Master, was very kind to create a new, darker version of the staff." Deku pointed the staff at me. "So tell me, Cora, do you remember the location of the staff now?"

"Well if you have your own version of the staff, then why do you need the real one? Surely, your master would have made this one superior?" I smirked at him, and he hissed in frustration.

"You really like to push my buttons, Cora. Don't you have any idea what this staff can do to you?"

"Alas, I don't, but that's a matter for later. Now, let's talk about you, Deku. How have you been? How is *the murderer* doing?" Deku opened his mouth, about to say something, but an ear splitting crash came from behind him as a tower of mops came tumbling out of the darkness on top of Deku. He fell to the ground and someone broke the chains that kept me bound to the chair. The person behind me grabbed my hand and we bolted down the hallway of what seemed to be a school. When the light of the windows lit the figure's face, I recognized him immediately.

"Oliver!?!" He turned to look over his shoulder at me as we kept running. Sure enough, it was Oliver, his green eyes flashing in the sunlight. "What are you doing?" I asked, astonished.

"Getting you out of here! The others will catch up."

"Others???"

We heard Deku scream, "AFTER THEM!" and I felt my blood turn to ice. Oliver led me down a long hallway and together we burst through a pair of double doors and out into an open courtyard.

CHAPTER 6

OLIVER - M.I.A

So, you're probably wondering: *how did you, Oliver, find Cora so quickly?*

It's because I'm totally awesome!!!

Yeah, that's actually not the case. Without the help of my friends, it would've been practically impossible to find Cora, but with Racheal's talents in forensics, Harper's ability to flirt, Cyrus' sneakiness, Fin's bravery in perilous situations, and a reckless person like me, we were the "dream team"! Let me explain how.

I shut the door behind me and got into my white Lincoln Navigator. I revved up the car and began to back out of the driveway just as Harper, Fin, Cyrus, and Racheal came barreling down toward me, opened the car doors, and squeezed in.

"What are you doing?" I asked.

"Coming with you, of course," Racheal said, exasperated. "What? Did you really think we were going to let you go find Cora on your own?"

"Well, no. But it's dangerous! You guys have no idea what you're getting yourselves into!"

"Well neither do you, Oliver! You're as oblivious to her location as we are. But if we all work together, I'm sure that we can find her." All of them looked at me and I smiled.

"Alright," I said. "We can all go, and I know where to start first." I hit the gas and the car sped out of the driveway and onto the road.

After twenty minutes of driving, we arrived at the hospital. Just like on the news, reporters were in the parking lot of the hospital where crowds of people were being pushed away by a S.W.A.T. team and police officers. As I watched, I saw firefighters, emergency responders, and another group of police officers wearing hazmat suits. They were carrying out bodies that seemed to be decaying on the spot. Some were even almost bone. I tried to get past a line of tape surrounding the building, but a police officer saw me and blocked my path.

"I'm sorry, kid, but you can't go past this point. Not unless you're one of us."

"My dad is the chief officer of Crystal Falls," Cyrus said. "Officer Miller? Surely you know him."

"Yes, he is here. Your father is investigating the situation, as we speak."

"Can we see him? My dad would let us in for sure."

"I wish I could, but I have strict orders from your father himself to not let anyone in."

"But we need to find our friend!" I argued.

"Don't worry, our autopsy will be able to identify the bodies. We're sorry for your loss though." The officer walked away and Harper put a hand on my shoulder.

"But we aren't looking for a body," I said. "We need to find Cora."

"We'll find her, Oliver. We just have to find another way."

"Guys!" Cyrus, Fin, Harper, and I turned to see Racheal inside the tape line surrounding the hospital. She was kneeling down to look at something marked on the concrete.

"What are you doing?" Fin asked, shocked. "Do you want to get arrested?" Racheal didn't respond. Instead, she snapped a photo of whatever she was looking at, ran over to us, and motioned to get back into our car. We got in and shut the door.

"What is it?" I asked her. Racheal pulled out her phone and showed us a photo of a long trail of tire marks leading from the hospital parking lot to the center of town.

"Tire marks. Judging by how the tire marks are really dark for at least a quarter of a mile, whoever was driving wanted to get as far away as they could before police arrived."

"You're the expert," Cyrus said, patting Racheal on the shoulder. "Tell us where to go."

"That way." She said enthusiastically, pointing east. I turned on the car and we sped away. We stopped here and there at shops, restaurants, and bus stops to see if anyone saw where the vehicle was going. After about thirty minutes, we arrived at a location that we never expected to be.

"Is that... our highschool?" Cyrus asked, shocked. Sure enough, we were driving into the back parking lot of Harriet Highschool. The glass windows surrounding the school glistened in the sunlight as we rolled to a stop behind a bunch of trash containers. Cyrus, Harper, Racheal and I got out of the car and looked around. About twenty feet away, a black Chevy was parked outside of the entrance to the school.

"That must be the vehicle that took Cora."

"Are you sure?" Harper asked.

"It's the same tire marks we've been following," Racheal said, looking at the tires on the vehicle. "This must have been where the kidnapper took her, but why to a school?"

"Well, it is the weekend," Cyrus said, shrugging.

"And it's a huge school that can easily hide people," Fin added.

"We can't worry about that now," I said, annoyed. "All that matters is how we get Cora out of there before it's too late." I ran toward Door 17 and grabbed the steel handles. I tried to yank the door open but with a loud rattle, it wouldn't budge.

"It's locked," I called over my shoulder.

"Well, how are we gonna get in?" Racheal asked.

"Harper, in the back of the Navigator, there is a tire jack. Can you pass it to me?"

Harper ran back to the Navigator, opened the trunk, and grabbed the jack before she handed it to me. "Here," she said, "But why would you..?" I swung the tire jack through the air, and it shattered the glass school door. Reaching through the broken glass, I unlocked the door from the inside.

"Oliver! Do you have any idea how many laws you just broke?"

"Well, if we don't find Cora, there probably aren't gonna be any laws left to break if the world ends!" I swung the door open, and together we all crept down the hallway, searching for any sign of Cora.

After an hour of searching hallways and classrooms, we still had half of the school to look through in order to find Cora. This was getting ridiculous! None of us ever realized how big Harriet High was! We finally sat down in the cafeteria and discussed what we found, which was nothing.

"We're never gonna find Cora!" Cyrus said in defeat. "This school is too big!"

"Maybe we should split up," I said, looking around. "If any of us find Cora, we can call each other on our phones."

"That could work," Racheal agreed. "But we have no idea what we're up against."

"Racheal's right," Harper added. "It's better that we stay in a group and-" A loud hissing seemed to whisper behind us, slowly getting louder and louder as a clump of shadows passed the windows in the cafeteria.

"Get down!" I whispered. We all hid under the lunch table and watched as a group of six men... Wait, they weren't exactly men. They were half man, half serpent, like they were relatives of Medusa. These "things" wore shiny dark armor, helmet and chest plate that glowed faintly the color of magenta. All of them were holding up the limp body of a girl with lush, brown hair and skin that was a slight beige color. She wore a long emerald green dress with a golden belt as well as a golden crown that looked like a wreath around her head. My heart seemed to melt from the flames of anger burning inside me.

"Is that Cora?" Harper whispered in my ear.

"Yeah," I said, clenching my fists under the table.

"Is she dead?" Fin asked.

"No," I said. "Her chest is moving like she's breathing."

"What are they going to do to her?" Racheal asked, her face pale in shock.

"I don't know. Either way we have to follow them." I waited until the monsters were out of sight before getting up and following them. We turned corners and went down hallways I never knew were even in the school. The group in front of me pressed a button that opened an orange colored garage door. Before we were too late, Cyrus, Fin, Harper, Racheal, and I slid baseball-style under the closing door.

The room was filled with a mix of dodgeballs, volleyball nets, mops, brooms, trash cans, and other cleaning supplies. We all hid behind a bunch of blue plastic barrels full of footballs and watched as the group of creatures placed Cora on a metal school chair and bound her hands behind the back of the chair with black chains that glowed purple. Once they were finished, they walked away into the darkness. It was silent for a moment before Cora stirred, looking surprised yet confused about where she was. She struggled to break free but stopped after a moment. Laughter echoed through the garage, making my hair stand on end. A creature, much more dangerous and muscular than the others, appeared from the darkness. He began to speak to Cora, but it wasn't in English. It was like a mix of Spanish, Latin, and Greek. She responded using the same language, which surprised me. She spoke it so fluently that it seemed to flow from her mouth like a waterfall.

"Oliver, come on," someone whispered behind me. The voice grabbed my shoulder and pulled me back closer to the others. Racheal, who was the one who grabbed me, looked at me with a curious but terrified expression.

"What are we going to do?" Fin whispered to me. All of them looked worried, waiting for me to give them an order like a commander to his troops in war. I looked back over my shoulder as Cora screamed in pain. Then, an idea came into my head.

"Alright," I whispered. "Here's what we have to do…"

After a few minutes, the plan was set. Cyrus grabbed a large bolt cutter and hid behind the volleyball nets near Cora. Fin climbed a ladder to get on top of a cabinet with an armful of mops. Racheal had knocked an arrow into one of the school's archery bows and drew back into position as Harper snuck out the back to distract one of the guards at the entrance. Only I, who had one simple job, was waiting behind a trash can to give the signal. We waited as the creature and Cora spoke to each other... One second... Two seconds...

I looked up and nodded to Fin. He nodded back, leaned over the cupboard, and dropped the tower of mops on top of the creature's head. It fell to the ground and I bolted forward. I heard a hiss from behind me as Racheal shot an arrow that missed my head and hit a creature in the shadows. Cyrus passed the bolt cutters to me and I broke Cora's chains, grabbed one of her hands, and sprinted out into the hallway. Out of the corner of my eye, I saw Harper flirting with a guard that was definitely more focused on Harper than what was going on around him.

"Oliver? What are you doing?" Cora asked, confused. I turned to look over my shoulder as we kept running.

"Getting you out of here! But don't worry, the others will catch up."

"Others???" From far away, we heard Deku scream, "AFTER THEM!", and I felt my blood turn to ice. I led Cora down a long hallway and together, we burst through a pair of double doors and out into an open courtyard.

"There's no time!" I told Cora. I unlocked the Lincoln Navigator's back door, got Cora inside, and turned on the car. It hummed to life, and I backed out of the parking lot.

"Wait!" Someone screamed from outside. I stopped the car as Harper, Racheal, Cyrus, and Fin bolted out the school doors and towards the car. They slammed the doors shut as they got in.

"GO!" Harper screeched. We sped out of the school parking lot and flew down the street. Even with the doors shut and nearly a mile away, we all shivered as a roar of anger echoed through the town of Crystal Falls.

CHAPTER 7

— ⁘ —

CORA - SECRETS OF THE STAFF

My jaw dropped when we arrived at Oliver's home. The U-shaped path that the car drove on led to what looked like a beautiful castle surrounded by a dense forest. It was made entirely of quartz, glinting fiercely against the sunlight. Sandstone was carved into two curved twenty-foot-tall stairways that lead to a dark oak door that was as tall as a giant. Beautiful arrays of flowers blossomed all around the entrance and a golden fountain in the shape of an eagle shot water high into the sunlight. The car stopped at the stairway, and we all got out. A man in a tux with his reddish gray hair smoothed back came forward, and Oliver gave him the car's starting mechanism that could fit in the man's hand.

"Max, please take the LN to the garage," said Oliver.

"Of course, Mr. Johnson," replied the man. Max then got into the car and drove off down another driveway that I didn't see before.

"Is that your knight?" I asked Oliver.

"Max? No, he's just one of our butlers. He helps around the house."

"Don't maids do that?"

"Cora, it's the twentieth century! Men and women have equal rights to do any job they think suits them."

I mouthed "twentieth century" as Oliver led the others and me into his house. The house was even more beautiful on the inside. He walked us up another flight of stairs, and brought us into his bedroom. We all sat down on Oliver's giant bed and Oliver introduced me to his friends that helped me escape. They all greeted me with a smile and a "it's very nice to meet you," but something about the girl's, Harper's, reaction made me freeze. Her smile looked almost fake and I could sense that for some reason, she didn't want me here. I didn't show it, but my feelings were a little hurt.

"So tell me," I said, looking at them all. "How long have I been gone? I know it's been a very, very long time because I don't ever remember seeing things like men being butlers instead of knights and a LN?"

"It's called a Lincoln Navigator," said Harper, sounding annoyed. "And you've been gone for over five hundred years."

"What?" My mind was racing. Sure, it explained a lot, but five hundred years?

"What doesn't make sense to me is how Cora looks our age," Fin said, looking at me. "Shouldn't you look old? Or dead?"

"My ancestor is Delphi. She was able to slow down her aging process because of her goddess blood. Because I'm a descendant, the same thing happens to me," I said calmly. Oliver and his friends stared at me in confusion. Even though it made perfect sense to me, I wasn't sure if their mortal brains could process what I had just said.

"Well," Cyrus said, "you're safe now, and that's what matters."

"Maybe Cora should leave now," Harper muttered. "Since she's supposed to be *so* powerful and all, surely she would be fine on her own." She sounded, I don't know, jealous perhaps?

"Harper! Be nice!" Cyrus scolded. Harper puffed in annoyance and walked out of the bedroom, her arms crossed. Everyone went silent, embarrassed by the crude comment made by Harper.

"So what are we going to do next?" Racheal asked, breaking the awkward silence. I looked around, taking in everything, when my eyes fell upon an old wooden stick that was carved with a small eagle perched on the top of the staff. Instantly, memory flashed before my eyes of an older boy's body lying on the ground, his hand clutching a tall staff made of gold that glowed brightly even in the darkness. On top, a hollowed out sun shaped spear head was molted to the staff. I came back to reality to see the others staring at me, their expressions worried.

"You ok, Cora?" Oliver asked. "You look like you saw a ghost."

"Yes," I said, trying to keep my voice calm. "And I know where to go." I cleared my throat, got up, and grabbed the wooden stick with my right hand. "There is a staff that was passed down in my family for countless generations. It was crafted for a young boy who was foretold to aid the goddess in the battle against Malice. This young boy later became the first king of Crystal Falls and the husband of Delphi."

"What did he do with the staff?" Cyrus asked me, getting up.

"Well, it was decreed that a person was chosen to wield the staff by the goddess Delphi through some sort of sign. My father chose a knight named Nick to carry the staff when I was born, but he died fighting Malice."

"That's terrible!" Racheal said.

"Yeah, but I'm guessing that it's somewhere on earth. I'm just not sure where." I looked around at them, trying to see what they were thinking. Harper poked her head in and looked at me as if I had gone crazy. Fin, Cyrus, and Racheal were looking at me in total fascination while Oliver was biting his lip, thinking.

"I think I might actually know where it is," he mumbled.

"What?" Cyrus asked. "How?" Oliver ran into his closet and came back moments later with a colored piece of paper that read, "Border State University: The place where all geologists start a bright future!" A symbol of a golden staff with a sun sticking out of a giant rock with people standing around it was plastered onto the sheet of paper.

"That's it!" I said, aghast. "How did you-?"

"It just looks like a staff that would be really powerful." Oliver shrugged.

"How are we supposed to find it?" Fin asked.

"We'll go to the college, and, because Oliver's trying to apply, he can get us in so we can find the staff and get out." Racheal said, confidently.

"Alright," I agreed. "When should we leave?"

"Tomorrow morning," Oliver said, looking out the window to see the sun going down. "It's getting late and we need sleep. We'll get up and leave at about ten-ish. Does everyone agree?"

We all nodded and got ready for bed. Oliver helped me find my way around the house and tried to make me comfortable. As he tried to make myself comfortable on the couch, I looked at him as my heart sank.

"Oliver?" I said.

"Yeah?"

"I'm so sorry about your grandfather. He- he was a very nice man." Oliver looked at me, his expression sad and mournful. He said, "thanks," but his voice caught before he could say anything else. I understood his pain. Losing a loved one is something that no one should have to go through.

I was the only one left awake when the moon had risen to its highest point. My brain was whirling in circles as memories continued to run through my head like horses running in a stable. No matter the cost, we had to get that staff. The outcome of the coming war between Malice and I, along with the fate of Crystal Falls and the entire world, was at stake.

CHAPTER 8

OLIVER - THE WRATH OF CORA

We left as soon as we could after the minor setback of having to find Cyrus' phone in between the sofa cushions. After that, we walked down the steps and out into the open sky. The sun danced across our faces as Max, my butler, pulled up in the Lincoln Navigator and handed me the keys.

"Thanks, Max," I said, smiling.

"No problem, sir." He whispered into my ear, "is that the girl from the..."

"News? Yeah," I said, matter of factly. He looked at me with a concerned expression on his face. You see, when my parents weren't around, Max was always there for me. Whether for advice or anything at all, he always wanted to help. He was like a second father to me. Max nodded, as to say: "I won't tell anyone" before walking away.

We all got into the car and drove onto the highway and out of Crystal Falls. We passed a giant sign that read: "Thanks for visiting!" before Fin broke the silence.

"Do you think that creature is looking for you?" he asked Cora.

"Not likely," she said confidently. Fin looked shocked at Cora's confidence and I felt the same. Even through everything that just happened, she looked as calm as can be, which didn't seem normal. But then, she'd been fighting Malice for five hundred years. It's probably in the "contract" to be calm when it comes to being her.

"How long does it take to get from here to Border State University?" Racheal asked.

"About an hour, so you might as well get comfortable." Racheal and Fin moaned dramatically before bursting into a fit of laughter. I looked in the rear view mirror to see Racheal take out her phone and begin to watch a video by Brent Miller while Cora, Fin, and Cyrus looked over her shoulder.

"Who's that?" Cora asked, pointing at the man

"Oh! That's Brent Miller, he's an amazing voice actor! I follow him on social media!"

"What is... social media?" Racheal began to explain to Cora about the cloud, the internet, and how social media works in a lot of detail though it still didn't look like Cora understood. I smiled a little. Cora looked kind of cute when she was confused...

"Oliver?" Harper whispered to me in the passenger seat. I jumped and had to jerk the car away before colliding into a jeep. They honked, but I ignored it.

"What?" I said, annoyed.

"Are we sure that Cora's sane?"

"Why would you even ask that?" I whispered.

"Well, there are a lot of reasons! She's wearing something that looks like it came from a movie. She's currently being hunted by people who look like they're relatives of Medusa, and now she's claiming that she's a descendant of the goddess we learned about at the museum. I mean, come on, Oliver! You honestly don't believe any of this, right?"

"Harper, look what we've been through. Look what I've been through." I pointed to a couple of stitches on my forehead and a long scar across my arm. "I have no doubt in my mind that Cora is who she said she is." I didn't go into further detail about Cora's voice and how she used to be in my head. That probably would've escalated things. Harper opened her mouth as if to protest, but I stopped her.

"Don't even start!" I said, loudly. Everyone went silent in the car and stared at Harper and I. Harper crossed her arms and muttered something about looking out for my self interest before biting her lip and going quiet.

We drove in silence for over an hour. By the time we arrived at the city where the university was, we were all hungry. Our stomachs were growling so loudly it sounded like angry animals. The city's skyscrapers stretched high above our heads as clusters of cars drove past us.

"Can we stop somewhere to eat?" Cyrus moaned.

"There's a drive thru down the street, but we'd have to walk. The traffic over there is too crazy." So in the end, I was able to park the car about a block away from the fast food restaurant.

We all got out of the car and breathed in the carbon dioxide that billowed out of the cars. I looked at Cora to see her reaction, but her expression looked blank.

"Let's go," I said, waving my hand for them to follow. Pigeons cooed and horns honked as we weaved our way through cars and people. The sky was growing dark as clouds formed above our heads. As we walked past an alleyway, a loud scream tore through the air, making us stop in our tracks.

"What was that?" Cora asked, looking down the dark alleyway.

"It's nothing. Probably just a group of kids fighting... Cora, wait!" But Cora had already disappeared into the darkness of the alley. We followed her and stopped when we saw a group of four teens huddled in a group. Two of the teens were holding the arms and legs of a young boy with skin that was so dark, he looked almost black. The third teen was punching and kicking the boy while the forth teen stood back, laughing and watching this all happen.

"What are they doing to him?" Cora said, aghast.

"They're beating him up," Racheal said, sounding disgusted.

"We have to help," Cora murmured. Before we could stop her, she took a few steps forward and shouted: "Hey! Leave him alone!"

The boys stopped what they were doing and turned to see who had spoken. The teenager who watched this all happen walked forward till he was arm's reach from Cora and looked down at her. He had sand colored hair that was buzzed military style. His eyes looked dilated, and his words slurred as he spoke like he was drunk.

"Now, who are you beautiful?"

"None of your business," Cora said, firmly.

"None of my business!?!" He said, frustrated.

"What are you doing to him?" Cora asked calmly.

"Beating up this piece of crap," the guy said.

"But why?"

"Because his kind don't belong!" he snarled. The color seemed to drain from Cora's face at the remark.

"That doesn't mean you have the right to hurt him," Cora argued.

"He's not white. He's a freak! His kind were created to serve us. They should've never been freed!" He walked back over to his friends and began to kick and punch the young boy, who screamed and wailed in agony.

"Might as well pick them off one by one," he called over his shoulder.

Suddenly, Cora's rage exploded from her. The dark alleyway filled with sunlight as waves of pure energy emanated from Cora, pulsing through our bodies like a tsunami crashing onto a sandy beach. I squinted in Cora's direction.

"Cora?" I said, astonished. She turned to look at me, and for a moment, I felt like I should kneel, submit, and obey her every order because I knew there was no way I could ever fight her and win. Cora then looked away and that feeling vanished immediately. She focused her gaze onto the group of boys and a lot of things happened at once. The group of teens holding the young boy let go of him and ran off, leaving their drunken defenseless leader at the mercy of Cora. She walked up to him, and he tried to back away, but Cora grabbed him by the shirt collar. With one hand, she lifted him up with the force of a bull and pinned him to the left alley wall.

"Now listen here," Cora growled, her voice echoing menacingly through the alley, even though she spoke quietly. "You will never harm anyone again. You will not criticize, bully, or terrorize people, whether they are like you or not... And if I find out you did something like this again, you will feel more pain than this young boy felt today. Do you understand?" The drunk teen nodded spastically before Cora let him go. He bolted away, stuttering apologies to the young boy as he passed. I walked forward and tenderly placed a hand on Cora's shoulder. The energy and light drained from Cora as she returned to her normal self.

"Was that your power?" I asked. She nodded.

"That was amazing!" Fin cheered. "You totally kicked their butts!"

"But why did you freak out so much?" I asked her. "Didn't your family have slaves five hundred years ago?"

"The laws of our kingdom decreed specifically that all people who walk on this earth shall be treated like family, no matter what they look like."

She took a few steps forward, knelt down, and held out her hand to the young boy.

"It's ok," Cora said softly. "What's your name?"

"Odion," the boy muttered.

"Doesn't that mean: 'First child of two twins?'" Cora asked. He nodded. "Where's your brother?"

"At home," Odion said. He took Cora's outstretched hand and she helped him up. Cora's body glowed, and we watched in awe as Odion's body healed. His skin reformed around some cuts on his arms and face, and the bruises on his body faded away, leaving unblemished skin. Odion's eyes grew wide.

"Thank you!" Odion said, sounding shocked at what had just happened.

"Go home and stay safe," she said to him. Odion nodded and ran off, disappearing around a corner. Cora walked back over to Racheal, Fin, Cyrus, Harper, and me silently. I put my arm around her shoulder, and she tensed, as if unsure what I was up to.

"Come on," I said to them all. "Let's go."

Before leaving, Harper stepped forward and, to all of our surprise, hugged Cora.

CHAPTER 9

CORA - WELCOME TO BORDER STATE UNIVERSITY

Oliver, Racheal, Harper, Fin, Cyrus, and I arrived at a place they called a restaurant and ordered our food, though Oliver had to help me figure out what to eat. Twenty minutes later, we left and walked back down the road the way we came. As we passed an old parking lot, we saw the same group of boys we met in the alleyway. They were smoking and drinking. When they saw me, their faces went white, and they clambered into a black vehicle before speeding out of sight. I shook my head in annoyance as we all got back into the car and continued our route towards Oliver's soon to be college.

About fifteen minutes later, we drove through metal gates that opened to a beautiful university. Five different buildings surrounded a lush, green park. Students were walking, playing games, and talking all around us. Oliver parked the car in front of the biggest building, which had a giant banner attached to the front of it saying: "WELCOME BACK CLASS OF 2025!" Large square windows were arranged in rows along the walls, shimmering with the reflection of the sun's rays.

As we walked across the street, there was definitely no denying that Oliver, Cyrus, Harper, Fin, and Racheal had never been on any type of mission before. Racheal kept muttering something about spy movies, whatever those are. Harper was fidgeting with her hands while Cyrus and Fin kept exchanging nervous glances. The only one that looked almost normal was Oliver. He walked alongside me, his hand every now and then brushing against mine, but I hardly noticed.

We walked up to a pair of double glass doors, and Oliver pressed a button which dinged the moment his finger made contact with it.

"Name and your reason for visiting, please?" I jumped in shock as a man's voice asked us the question.

"Oliver Johnson, and I'm here with a few of my friends for a school tour."

"Come in," the right door clicked open, and Oliver held open the door, allowing us inside.

"How did that door talk?" I asked.

"Someone at the front desk has a camera and microphone that's wired to that button I just pushed so they can talk to me." Oliver explained everything very quickly. I nodded in understanding even though I had no clue what he meant. We got passes from the security guard and walked down two hallways before Oliver led us into a classroom. He locked the door, and he, Cyrus, Fin, Harper, and Racheal turned to look at me.

"Okay, Cora," Oliver said. "What's the plan?"

"What?"

"Well, you know where the staff is, right?" Cyrus asked.

"I think so. I mean, I've had some sort of buzzing in my ears and..." I rubbed my head, a little annoyed. "It just won't stop."

"So, if we get closer to the staff, then you'll know?" Harper asked. I nodded.

"It's like a homing beacon," Fin said, smiling. We all rolled our eyes.

"Ok," Racheal said. "Oliver, you pretend to be a tour guide that's taking us around the school. We'll follow, and if Cora feels something different, we'll follow that direction. Everyone got it?"

Everyone nodded in agreement. Then, we got into a small cluster. Oliver led us in the front while I was surrounded by the others, leaving me in the center. We walked around the university for about an hour before something happened. As we walked down a hallway that had a sign reading "Administration Offices", the buzzing in my ears became a high pitched screech that made me double over and cover my ears.

"It's in there," I said, pointing toward the door. Suddenly, a man wearing a suit and blue tie walked up to us, smiling. His dark black hair was neatly combed to one side and his face seemed to light up in delight when he saw us, but immediately I knew something was wrong. The air around us seemed to grow unnaturally peaceful and calm. I could sense Oliver, Racheal, Fin, Cyrus, and Harper beginning to relax as they swayed on the spot.

"Good afternoon!" said the man. "I'm Professor Zombone, but you can call me Professor Z." Professor Z stretched out his hand, and Cryus, in a daze, shook it. Immediately, his body seized up and he froze like a statue; the others seemed to not notice. One by one, Harper, Fin, and Racheal shook hands with the professor and froze into statues just like Cyrus. When Oliver walked up and was about to shake hands with Professor Z, I got in between them.

"I'm sorry, but we don't shake hands," I said, gritting my teeth.

"Oh, don't you now?" Professor Z said. Two doors, one to our right and one to our left opened, revealing ten other professors wearing the same outfit as Professor Z was. They all marched over and surrounded Oliver and I. Two grabbed our shoulders, and every muscle in my body stiffened as a great tiredness fell upon me like a soft blanket. My vision blurred, and I fell unconscious.

Next thing I knew, I woke up, bleary eyed, being carried with Oliver, Cyrus, Fin, Harper, and Racheal in the professors' arms down a dark underground passageway. As we traveled farther and farther down into the earth, I tried not to scream in horror as I watched the professors' flesh begin to rot to reveal muscle, tendons and bones. One turned it's head like an owl's to look at me, and I almost screamed when I saw it's face. One eye was dangling out of the left socket and half of his face was missing, leaving nothing but bone. When I looked to my left, I saw Oliver looking right back at me. He mouthed, "You can get us out of here, right?"

I didn't answer because, honestly, I had no clue if my power would do any good against the undead.

Soon, Cryus, Harper, Fin, and Racheal were awake and looking absolutely terrified. They struggled with all of their might, trying to break free, but it was no use. The undead professors may not look strong, but their grip was like an iron vise.

After what seemed to be days later, we finally passed through the end of the tunnel and into some kind of light. I shielded my eyes before looking to see where we were. A large cavern plagued with stalactites and stalagmites opened before us. Bats zoomed over our heads and through varying tunnels to our right, left, and back the way we came. As the undead warriors plopped us down next to each other against one side of the cavern wall, they cuffed our hands and feet with chains. We tried to break them, but even I knew that it wasn't going to help. We wouldn't be able to escape.

At least not yet...

The undead Professor Z. pulled out a small, rectangular device and began to speak into it, his teeth clicking.

"He's using a walkie talkie," Oliver muttered.

"What are we going to do?" Harper whimpered.

"Maybe they'll eat our brains?" Cyrus said, trying to make some kind of joke.

"Cyrus, this is not a good time!" Fin snapped. A zombie woman turned to look at us and hissed in annoyance, making Cyrus and Fin go silent. I looked over at Oliver and the others. I mouthed, "Get ready to run."

Professor Z. stopped talking to the walkie talkie and walked over to us, his face morphing back into its human appearance before he began to speak.

"Alright, listen up. Our master is coming, and before that, we have to ask you a couple of questions. If you guys play nice and answer truthfully, we won't have to do this the hard way. Got it?" We all nodded though in the back of my mind, I was counting down from five... four... three... two... one...

"Go!" I cried. I used my power to break the chains binding me and my friends. They shattered into dust, and we bolted for the exit passageway to our left. The undead scattered as I sent an arc of light at them, making a couple of unlucky professors disintegrate on the spot.

"Let's get out of here!" Fin yelled. Just before Oliver and I could follow, as we were the last two to run through the exit, a wall of fused bones erupted from the ground, blocking our path.

"Racheal! Fin! Cyrus! Harper! Go! We'll try to find another way out!"

But that was a lie. The rest of the undead professors were now closing in on us as more zombies, wearing all sorts of armor followed in pursuit.

"Well," said Professor Z. "I guess we're going to do this the hard way."

CHAPTER 10

—— ❋ ——

OLIVER - THE SHORT CHAPTER: A MENTAL NOTE BY OLIVER JOHNSON

Dear Me,

How did I get to be a part of this?

I mean, I'm Oliver Johnson. I'm just a normal teenager... Right? Why of all people am I destined to help Cora; a girl who has gone through so much pain and suffering? I can't even imagine what it's like to be her! I don't deserve such a privilege to be with her.

I'm sorry if I fail you, Cora. I care for you more than you will ever know. You mean everything to me and I want you to know that your happiness and safety is my top priority.

But, who am I kidding? You'll never see or hear this little mental note.

CHAPTER 11

—— ◆ ——

CORA - THE RETURN OF MALICE

Oliver and I held our breaths as the undead warriors dunked our heads into barrels of water. My brain was spinning as my ears, mouth, and nose flooded with water. I felt as if I wanted to scream, but I knew it was no use. No one would hear me. I counted in my head as the blood pounded in my ears. *Seventeen... Eighteen... Nineteen...* A hand clasped my neck and pulled me out of the water, and I was shoved to the ground. I heard Oliver's body thud to the ground next to me. One undead soldier, wearing a golden helmet, flipped me over to face him and put the tip of a spear on the center of my neck. His jaw bobbed up and down as his worn down teeth clicked against themselves. Even though what they were saying probably didn't make sense to Oliver, it made complete sense to me.

"Who we are is none of your business," I said, calmy. The undead warrior hissed in anger and raised the spear as if to strike.

"Cora, I wouldn't antagonize him if I were you..." Oliver said. Another undead warrior, this time dressed in a camouflaged soldier's outfit, slapped its bony hand across the right side of Oliver's face, making a loud **THWACK**! He yelped. Instinctively, I flicked one of my hands toward the warriors, who went flying backwards from the light wave that flew from my fingertips. After that, there was an eruption of chaos and fighting. An army of undead warriors surged up from the ground and launched spears and swords into the air towards Oliver and I. I created a forcefield around us, protecting me and Oliver from harm.

"STOP!!!" A voice which sounded like a roaring lion echoed through the cave, making my brain vibrate in my skull. The air around us seemed to become hard to breathe in as if all the oxygen was being sucked out. I lowered the shield surrounding Oliver and me and we looked in the direction where the voice came. A tall figure, dressed in a long eggplant purple robe with black, dead vines that weaved in and out of the fabric moved towards us. But that wasn't the most disturbing thing. It was the face of the thing that now stood before us. His face looked melted and deformed like it was put into a fire. Two magenta eyes with slit pupils like a snake's bulged out of his face as black matter swirled around him. When he saw us, his eyes immediately met mine, and a fountain of memories sprouted in my mind. They were so fast that the only thing I recognized was the thing that stood before me and his name.

"You..." It said in a hissing voice, his eyes dilating.

"Malice," I said, gritting my teeth. He began to circle Oliver and me like a vulture looking down at a dead carcass. He grabbed my chin with his black, dead looking hand. He tilted my head from side to side.

"I thought I had finished you when I escaped." Another memory flashed in my mind of Malice attacking me, and suddenly, my anger and hatred of Malice seemed to erupt from me. Malice hissed like an angry cat as he recoiled from the power and light that emanated from my body. He looked at me, and I could tell that his fury was boiling up inside him.

"Impudent little girl. I will easily defeat you as I have done before. However, this time... I will finish you!"

Malice held out his hand, and a ball of black fire appeared. He raised it high into the air and threw it straight at my face.

"Cora, look out!" Oliver pushed me aside, and the fire hit him square in the face. He yelled in pain and fell to the ground, writhing.

"No!" I tried to get up and run toward him, to help him, but I was blasted back as if by an invisible force. The back of my head hit the rock wall behind me, and I slid to the ground in a daze.

"Now Cora," Malice said, his voice becoming stronger. "I will finish you once and for all!" He pointed toward Oliver and a terrible dread seemed to spread from my head to my fingertips as I watched Oliver's body become still, get up and turn to face me. He looked like himself, except for his eyes. They weren't their normal olive green. Instead, they looked just like Malice's.

"Oliver?" I asked, terrified. He hollered a war cry and lunged for my throat. Before I could react, he was choking me with one hand and punching me in the solar plexus with the other. I tried to gasp for air and sent a jet of light at Oliver, hitting him squarely in the chest. He let go and flew back about twenty feet. Blood ran down the corner of his mouth as he got up, groaning. I staggered to my feet and winced as my body was electrified with pain. I felt blood trickling down the back of my head, and my vision went a little blurry. I watched as Oliver, using the power of Malice, made two double edged swords materialize into his hands. He swung them around as he ran at me and slashed down, trying to slice me into bacon, but I dodged and sent another jet of light at Oliver, missing his left ear by an inch. My knees gave out, and I collapsed onto the ground. I heard Malice roar with laughter at the sight of me getting tired.

What is wrong with me? I should easily be able to defeat Oliver! He's only a mortal.

But that was it. That's what was wrong.

For some reason, Malice knows that I wouldn't hurt Oliver.

"Admit it, Cora, you're too weak," Malice said, smiling down at me. "Your demise is now." I could hear my heart beating fast, my hatred flaring up inside me as I pushed myself up and looked Malice dead in the eye.

"Never."

"Fine. If you're going to be *so* obstinate." He pointed to me. Out of the corner of my eye, I saw Oliver's body stand to attention. "Oliver, finish her." Oliver and I turned to face each other, but my heart seemed to drop as I saw the hatred and resentment in Oliver's expression. He dropped his swords and his fists became flaming black fire balls.

"Oliver, no!" but he lunged.

That was when I probably did the stupidest thing I could ever do in my life. I grabbed both of Oliver's wrists and thrust them into the air, leaving us in a standoff. Oliver roared in frustration, and as he spoke, his voice seemed different as if there were three of him talking at once.

"Let go of me, Cora! I serve Malice!"

"Oliver, look at yourself! This isn't you!" Oliver struggled and tried to break free of my grasp. But I dug my nails into his wrists to keep from losing my grip, trying to ignore the terrifying feeling of the flames in Oliver's hands burning my own.

"Oliver, listen to me! I know you're in there! You have to fight it!" A mysterious wind seemed to whip around us as our two opposing forces were molded together as each tried dominating the other. By now, the power and light emanating from me was nearly turning the world around us a bright color of gold, but that only made me become more tired.

"Fight it, Oliver!" I yelled over the wind, sliding back a couple of inches. "I can't do this alone! I need you! I need Oliver Johnson!"

Oliver looked into my eyes, and for a moment, his eyes looked normal.

"I..." He relaxed and collapsed onto my chest, making me fall backwards.

"No!" Malice's anger made his voice reverberate around the cave as he looked at me with a surprised and hatred etched across his face. "He may have failed, but I will not let you get away again!" Malice dove down at Oliver and me. With all of my remaining strength, I made us disappear in a flash of light, leaving the fury of Malice behind us as his scream of anger filled our ears.

CHAPTER 12

—— ◆ ——

OLIVER - THE NEWCOMERS

When I opened my eyes, all I could see was golden light around me with Cora's body pressing against mine as the world around us closed in. Then, we appeared in front of Harper, Cyrus, Fin, and Racheal. For a moment, they all stood there in shock and silence before Cora passed out, I caught her in my arms before she hit the ground. That's when my friends turned around and ran forward to help set Cora down.

"Oliver! Are you guys ok?" Harper asked. "What happened?"

"Cora... She just saved my life... Malice possessed me and she was able to snap me out of it and get us here." As I spoke, I placed the palm of my hand onto Cora's forehead and instantly regretted it. The heat from Cora's skin felt like a thousand suns, making my hand feel like it was melting. I yelped and jumped back, checking to see if my hand was still intact. "She's burning up... Literally."

"Fin, Harper, and I will go and try to find some underground stream or water source," Racheal said, pointing to herself then the other two. "Oliver and Cyrus, you guys stay here and keep an eye on Cora.

Whatever you do, don't leave this spot. We don't want the possibility that we all get separated again."

Cyrus and I nodded and together Fin, Harper, and Racheal walked out of the open area we were in and into the darkness, using their phones as a source of light. I fidgeted with my hand and kept giving nervous glances in Cora's direction. Cyrus must have noticed because he nudged my shoulder and said, "She's gonna be ok, Oliver. She's strong."

We waited for what seemed to be an hour, and by then Cora was only getting worse. Her skin was now pale with red blotches, and her breathing was becoming more shallow and ragged every minute. I dared not touch her. There was no way I wanted to get a third degree burn, but something glinted out of the corner of my eye. It was a locket molded into the shape of a heart on Cora's chest. I'd never noticed her wearing it before. I knelt down and unhooked the chain from her neck. I had to "hot potato" it in my hands for about a minute from the heat it collected from Cora before Cyrus, who had come over to see what I was up to, and I were able to get a closer look at it. Cyrus turned on his phone's flashlight so we could see it. It looked like a regular locket. I flipped it over, and we could see writing engraved neatly onto the back of it.

"*To the best sister ever:*

Be yourself!

Love,

Grace"

"Who's Grace?" Cyrus asked, looking confused.

"Cora's little sister..." Together, we carefully opened up the locket. Inside there was a beautiful photo of a younger Cora, much like the one at the museum, laughing while hugging a little girl about the age of five. The little girl wore a white little dress with a bunch of lotus flowers sewed into the fabric here and there. She had red hair that looked like fire in the light, and her eyes were the color of emeralds.

"They look so happy," Cyrus said, sounding a little wistful. I nodded in agreement and closed the locket with a soft click. Suddenly, the locket glowed brightly in the darkness, and I shielded my face with one of my hands. The light dimmed, and I looked down to see something that made the hair stand up on the back of my neck. Words were slowly being engraved into the front of the locket like a ghost was writing it.

"Oh my..." I said. I looked at Cyrus, whose mouth was in the shape of an "O".

"What does it say?" Cyrus said. I began to speak, and in the back of my mind, I felt as if I heard a woman's voice. One that I have never heard before like a soft, gentle breeze.

"The child shall earn it,

For better or worse.

But take a step further,

A blessing and curse.

Call upon the sun that cries,

And you shall see the Temple rise.

Destroyed with the child's final breath.

They shall lose her to worse than death."

On the last word, the air around us suddenly grew cold. My heart seemed to tighten in dread of what all of the words could possibly mean.

"What does it mean by: 'take the step further?'"

"And 'they shall lose her to worse than death?'" I asked. Cyrus and I looked over at Cora with anxious expressions.

"If this prophecy is about Cora," Cyrus began. "What if it means-?" A shuffling of multiple footsteps interrupted Cyrus as the noise came towards us. Cyrus pointed his phone's flashlight to where the sound came from, but no one was there. Then, everything went quiet.

"Who's there?" I called out to the darkness. No response. Then suddenly, six figures circled around us, all wearing golden armor and wooden dragon masks painted in different colors to cover their faces like Hawaiian tiki masks. Each was also carrying an assegai spear made of some sort of dark marble.

"What the!?!" Cyrus yelped. I shushed him and walked forward, putting my hands up to show that I didn't want to fight.

"Hello," I said, my voice cracking a little. "I'm Oliver. We come in peace. We don't want to..." Suddenly, one person in a mask took out a handful of powder from a satchel around his shoulder and blew it into Cyrus' face.

"Hey!" Cyrus coughed. "That wasn't n-!" But his voice slurred, and he collapsed onto the ground. The same masked guy blew another handful of power. This time into my face.

"What the? What is this stuff?" But before they could answer, my vision went dark, and I passed out.

When I woke up, I found myself bound once again next to Cryrus, Harper, Fin, and Racheal. Four masked people stood around us with spears with their backs turned to face me.

"Oliver," Harper whispered. "Thank goodness you're awake."

"How did they get you?" I asked.

"They caught us by surprise as we turned a corner in a passageway. We didn't

even have time to react."

"Where's Cora?"

"Over there. Two of them are trying to wake her. Though, I don't know how they're going to when she's still unconscious."

About twenty feet away, Cora lay motionless on the rocky ground. Two masked people were walking around her. One wore a golden dragon mask with a laurel around its horns. The other wore a normal wooden mask but had large colored feathers covering the top of the mask like a lion's mane. Even though the two seemed to be whispering, I could still make out what they were saying to each other.

"She is the one, Chayton," the golden dragon masked person said in a deep, masculine voice. The other masked man nodded and gestured for one of the masked soldiers next to me to come forward.

"Haki!" Chayton yelled. The soldier, Haki, ran forward and knelt down before him. "Put her back with the others."

"Yes, Chayton," Haki said. He picked Cora up like a sack of potatoes and carried her over to where my friends and I sat, plopping Cora down next to me. I nudged Cora.

"Cora," I whispered. "Cora, wake up!" Her eyes fluttered open.

"Oliver! Oh thank goodness you're alright!"

"Not so loud!" I said as one of the guards looked over his shoulder to see us talking before looking away. Cora looked around, confused.

"Where are we?"

"I'm not sure," I said. Cora looked down at the ropes tied around her wrist. She must have spotted something like a sharp rock because she leaned down and began to rub her wrists onto the ground. The sound of the scuffing of the ropes must have annoyed Haki because he whipped around and pointed his spear at Cora's shoulder. But Cora didn't notice.

"Enough." He jabbed Cora's shoulder lightly with his spear as if to warn her. A small trickle of blood dribbled down her torn sleeve from where the spear pierced her skin.

"Ow! Watch it!" Cora snarled. Her eyes turned from electric blue to gold and her body began to emanate a fierce, golden light that nearly blinded everyone. Haki and the other soldiers took a few steps back in horror and amazement. They watched in wonder as Cora's wound healed itself instantly. Then Cora returned to normal, taking a deep breath to try and calm down.

"Are you ok?" I asked. She nodded. Haki looked at both of us in utter disbelief. Then he helped Cora and I up and led us down another passageway to the entrance of a small cavern about the size of a school classroom. Chayton stood there, protecting the entrance.

"What is it, Haki?" Chayton asked.

"These two were making noise. Then this girl started glowing and he-" Chayton silenced him with a wave.

"Is this true?" Chayton asked Cora. After a moment's pause, she nodded. "Haki, leave her and her friend here."

"But Chayton..." Haki began.

"Return to your post!" Chayton ordered. Haki huffed and walked away.

"Come with me," Chayton said, leading us inside. In the center of the cavern stood the golden masked person, who seemed to be the leader of the group. His back was turned to us, but when he heard us walk in, he turned around. Chayton knelt down before him, not saying a word.

"You have come a long way."

"What do you want with us?" Cora snarled.

"You wear the symbol of the Royal Family of Crystal Falls," he said, pointing at the crown on Cora's head.

"Yes, I do. Why do you ask." The guy in the golden mask stared at Cora. I looked at Cora and could see that her blue eyes were flickering from gold to blue then back to gold.

"Who are you?" The leader asked Cora. For a moment, Cora looked as if she was contemplating whether to tell the truth or not. Finally, she sighed as if in defeat.

"My name is Cora Williams. I am the daughter of Queen Emiliy and King Herald of the Kingdom of Crystal Falls as well as the descendant of Delphi, the goddess of the sun." The leader stood before her in stunned silence. Then he began to unstrap his mask, making loud clicks.

"Sire," Chayton said, getting up in protest. "I wouldn't. Our creed states..." But he stopped as his leader took off his mask. The leader was a lot younger than what I was expecting, maybe a year older than Cora and I. He had tan skin and straight black hair. His face had chiseled features and gray eyes like a bullet. His eyebrows were knitted together, giving him an expression of deep thought. Face paint was lined along his face where his cheekbones, chin, and forehead were.

"Who are you?" Cora asked.

"I'm Prince Dakota. We've been waiting for a long time to meet you, Cora."

"We?"

"The Tribe of the Rising Sun, of course! I'm sure your mother has told you about us?"

"I... uh... no... uh..." Cora stammered. Then her body snapped to attention. "Wait. You knew my mother?"

"Well, no," Prince Dakota said. "But my father told me about your family. All of the ancestors of Delphi come to this mountain to seek the Tribe's help to destroy Malice after receiving their blessing." I looked at Cora, whose mouth was open in shock.

"I... I don't understand." Suddenly, Haki came running in, carrying his spear and wearing a grimace on his face.

"Shall I execute them, sire?"

"Haki!" Chayton said, looking aghast. "What nonsense are you talking about!?! These are our guests!"

"Guests? Chayton, these are trespassers on our land! It is against our laws not to execute them!" Prince Dakota and Chayton stepped in front of Cora and I, ready to protect us.

"It is not against our laws if these trespassers are Delphi's descendant and her protectors," Prince Dakota said, keeping his voice calm. Haki stood there, silent. When he opened his mouth to argue, Chayton cut him off.

"Haki! A word." As a group, Haki, Chayton, and Prince Dakota walked away from Cora and I as they began to argue with one another.

"They know who you are?" I whispered. Cora shrugged as we watched Haki stomp off back through the exit the way he came.

"We're sorry for Haki and everyone's harsh behavior." Chayton said, walking over with Prince Dakota and untying the ropes around our wrists.

"It's alright," Cora said. "Your laws were set in place to protect your tribe."

"But all the same," Prince Dakota said. "We are sorry for our actions." He held out his hand as if offering it to Cora. "Please come with us." Cora took it and for a second, I saw her cheeks flush red. That, for some reason, really annoyed me.

"We appreciate your offer, your highness," I began, "but we really need to get..." Cora slapped a hand over my mouth and looked at me directly in the eyes.

"It's ok, Oliver," she said to me, deliberately. "We can go with them. After all, they're supposed to help us." I rolled my eyes and nodded in defeat.

Prince Dakota smiled and clapped his hands together. "Well! I'm very glad you've had a change of heart, Oliver."

"But what about our friends?" I asked, pointing in the direction where Racheal, Cyrus, Fin, and Harper were, being kept out of sight.

"I will inform the guards that your friends will come as well and must be treated as guests, not trespassers," Chayton said. "Wait here." He ran off, returning moments later with our friends, who were no longer wearing ropes around their wrists. Haki and the other guards quietly followed behind. Harper, Racheal, Cyrus, and Fin turned to look at me, as if seeking reassurance that we could trust them. I gave them a thumbs up to let them know we're all good.

"Alright," Prince Dakota said, "Now that we're all here, let's go."

CHAPTER 13

$\text{---} \diamond \text{---}$

CORA - THE TRIBE OF THE RISING SUN

Oliver, Racheal, Cyrus, Harper, Fin, and I followed Prince Dakota, Haki, Chayton, and the other guards as they led us down multiple passageways and tunnels. During that entire time, Prince Dakota and Oliver stood on either side of me, every now and then letting their hand nudge mine as if trying to say, "I'm here for you." Once, when we had to crawl through a tiny tunnel, Prince Dakota offered to help me up, and I could sense Oliver's annoyance as I accepted Dakota's hand.

After about an hour of walking, we arrived at a dead-end with a smooth, rock wall blocking our path.

"Uhh," Cyrus said. "How are we supposed to get through?"

"Princess Cora," Dakota said. "May I have your hand once more?"

"Of course," I said. He smiled as his soft hand gently grabbed mine. Dakota guided me to the wall, and I followed. He placed my hand against the cold, stone wall. Light broke from the stone and carved its way through it, tracing around my hand and I lept back in shock.

"Hey, it's ok," Prince Dakota said. "Look." I watched as the light began to spread and curl its way to every corner of the stone, creating symbols and markings. Then, the light faded.

"So, what now?" Fin asked.

"You go through," Chayton muttered. I looked at him then reached out my arm once more to touch the rock... But my hand went through. We all gasped in amazement. I walked through the rock wall and found myself in cascading light. When my eyes adjusted, I found myself in a giant, and I mean giant, opening in a cave that seemed to be as big as the earth above. Rows and rows of tents made out of varying material circled around a huge castle made out of quartz. Golden roof shingles lined the tower tops. I took in the scenery astounded by how big the space was. Within a few moments, everyone else followed behind me.

"Welcome to the Tribe of the Rising Sun," Chayton announced.

"Come on!" Prince Dakota said. "My family and tribe will be pleased to finally meet you." He led us into the Tribal village and past a bunch of small, open tents and markets, full of an abundance of fruits, meats, and jewelry. Children wrapped in cloth and furs scurried around us and in between tents, squealing as they played tag. One little girl bumped into my leg and looked up at me.

"Sorry, ma'am," the girl said. Then she saw my crown and her eyes widened, "Oh my Delphi! You're-"

"Shh!" Prince Dakota said, hushing the child. "Go, and don't tell anyone yet, ok?" The young girl nodded and ran off to catch up with her friends as we continued down the main path towards the castle. As we entered, two rows of guards stood on either side of the gate. When they saw Chayton, they pounded their right hand against their chest and knelt down before Prince Dakota. But when they saw the rest of us, they began to look at each other and whisper in earnest.

"Could it be? Her... After all this time..?"

"Hey!" Chayton's voice boomed, and every guard went quiet. "These are our guests. Treat them with dignity and respect."

"Yes, General Chayton!" the guards replied in unison. We continued walking through the castle halls on red velvet carpet until we were in front of two golden doors as tall as a house. Two guards, wearing dragon masks and gold armor, bowed their heads briefly in acknowledgement of our presence before opening the doors to reveal a large throne room. Lamps and torches illuminated the room and reflected off the walls and suits of armor the guards were wearing. Guards were scattered around the outer edges of the throne room. The long red carpet continued and led up to five thrones made of wood with gold paint on them. Four out of five thrones were occupied by people; I could tell that they must be related because each looked similar to one another. For one, most of them had tan skin.

The two smallest thrones were occupied by two girls. One, who looked about the age of four, had short black hair that barely reached her shoulders, and she had eyes like a hawk, yellow and serious looking, but her smile gave away the fact that she must be really friendly. Her smile could have made the flowers on the earth's surface dance off into the sunset. The second girl, about the age eleven, had long curly black hair that was braided to go over her right shoulder. She had gray eyes, just like Prince Dakota, but she didn't smile. Instead, she looked at me with fleeting glances and then would look back down at her hands. Both girls wore long, white silk dresses and a golden necklace with a small bird's skull attached to it. The third smallest throne was slightly larger than the two smaller ones. It was unoccupied, so I guessed it was Prince Dakota's. On the second largest throne sat a beautiful woman. Unlike the rest of her family, she had pale, white skin and honey blonde hair with silver streaks mixed in here and there. Her eyes were gray, just like her son and daughter, and wrinkles lined the corners of her eyes to show she must smile a lot. She wore a long wolf skinned dress with a belt made of leather and bone. A crown of vines and flowers encircled her head. Finally, in the largest throne sat a burly man who looked like he could squash me and my friends with only his pinky. He was tall with shaggy black hair and tan skin that stretched across his muscular body. He had yellow eyes like his youngest daughter and chiseled features like his son. He wore armor made of gold as well as a fur cape that draped over the arm of his throne. Spikes made of fused bone were attached to the shoulders of the cape and stuck up behind the man. He wore a crown that was made out of bat bones. As we walked forward, the man's arms stretched out in welcome.

"Dakota, my boy!" His voice boomed. "How are you, son? How was the hunt?" Then he caught sight of us. "It seems to me that you've brought something home other than food."

"Indeed I have, father!" Prince Dakota said, smiling. "These are my friends: Oliver,Racheal, Fin, Cyrus, Harper, and Cora Williams. My friends, this is my father, Ansel, chief of the Tribe." Chief Ansel didn't say anything at first. Instead, he looked at me with a look of great confusion and disbelief.

"You are Cora Williams?" Chief Ansel asked, pointing at me. I nodded. For a moment, he was silent before he broke into a smile and began to laugh.

"Thank the Tribe that you are here at last! We've been waiting so long to meet you! Please, let me introduce you to my family. This is my wife, Chieftess Neenah; it means 'running water.' And these are my children." Chief Ansel gestured to Prince Dakota and his two daughters. "You already know my son, Prince Dakota. His name means 'ally' or 'little bear.' And these are my two daughters. The older one is Princess June, which is Latin for 'young in spirit.' And this is my youngest daughter, Princess Lara. It is Latin meaning 'the lovely citadel' or 'the cheerful one.'" They all waved to me and I waved back politely.

"Wait, so does everyone's name here have meaning?" Oliver asked Chief Ansel.

"Indeed, sir..."

"Oliver. Oliver Johnson." Oliver said, straightening up as he was addressed as a "sir."

"Well, yes," Chief Ansel said. "Each name was given to us after the age of five by Delphi when we finally became part of the Tribe. My name, Ansel, means 'the protector'. My job as chief is to protect the tribe. General Chayton's name means 'the eagle' because he is wise and will protect anyone at any cost much like an eagle protecting its young. Haki's name means 'ambition' and 'will power.'"

"Chief Ansel," I said. "May I ask a question."

"Yes."

"Does my name have any meaning?"

"Of course it does. Every name has a meaning, though it's sometimes not acknowledged."

"What is it?"

"The name, 'Cora', means 'heart of a maiden'. Your mother, Emily, chose that name for you."

"Do you know why?" I asked hopefully. Chief Ansel shook his head.

"Only your mother knew. My ancestors never said why she chose that name for you. Only that she thought it would suit you." I nodded, even though I felt my heart sink in disappointment that he didn't know. "But now," Chief Ansel continued, addressing everyone, "We must prepare a celebration in honor of you and your protectors' arrival. Princess Lara, Princess June, please escort Cora and the other maidens to the guest room on the fourth floor. Prince Dakota, escort the boys to the third floor guest room." Prince Dakota and his sisters nodded and we parted ways. Prince Dakota and the boys went through the left hallway while Princess Lara, Princess June, Harper, Racheal, and I headed down the right hallway and up the stairs.

CHAPTER 14

OLIVER - FEELINGS

Prince Dakota led Cyrus, Fin, and I up three flights of stairs where he brought us to another pair of large double doors with two guards wearing dragon tiki masks guarding the entrance. They knelt before Prince Dakota. Then, they got up and opened the doors to reveal a bedroom that was bigger than mine at the mansion. That's saying something because my bedroom was the entire third floor! The room was very vast and open with nine foot windows that led to a balcony on the right side and a bed and closet to the left. At the end of the room was a door with the words "bathroom and showers" engraved above it.

"Make yourself at home," Prince Dakota said. "The feast will probably start in an hour, knowing my father. I'll come and get you when it is time." He turned around and left. Cyrus, Fin, and I decided to take showers and get ready. I flopped onto the bed as soon as I had finished. Fin stopped what he was doing and sat down next to me. Without any warning, he punched me in the shoulder.

"Ow! What the heck was that for?"

"That was for you not being honest with yourself," Fin said.

"What are you talking about?" I asked, my teeth gritted as I messaged my arm.

"You like Cora," Fin teased, smiling.

"What!?! No! She's not my type!"

"Bro, you always look at her with those googly eyes. You would do anything you can to keep her safe, and you were practically trying to show dominance to Prince Dakota by staying less than three inches away from Cora!"

"Our job is simple, Fin: to protect Cora," I said defensively. "Besides, she's part goddess and has royal blood! I don't even know if her laws allow her to date people who don't have the same status."

"So, you're saying that if those laws weren't there, you'd ask Cora out?"

"Fin!" Fin laughed and rolled off the bed with a loud thud, making me roar in laughter as Cyrus came out in his clothes as he rubbed a towel on his wet hair.

"Did you know they have a plumbing system down here?" Cyrus asked, sounding shocked. "I mean, they're like two hundred feet below sea level!" Then he saw Fin's smiling face and raised an eyebrow. "What's going on?"

"Oh we're talking about Oliver's fascination over Cora and how he's in denial about it," Fin joked.

"Gee... Thanks Fin," I said, rolling my eyes. "And it's not a fascination! Sure, she's beautiful, and her smile makes the day seem brighter, and her hair is always perfect, and her skin is..." That's when I went into a daze and imagined Cora's soft, white hand holding mine as we sat on the balcony of my parent's mansion looking out onto a beautiful sunset. Her other hand was holding my face as we leaned in to kiss... Suddenly, my stomach seemed to drop as I snapped to realization and reality. "Oh my gosh!" I said, my mouth drying. "I'm in love with Cora Williams."

"Finally!" Cyrus and Fin said in unison, both rolling their eyes. Then there was a knock on the door, and Prince Dakota came in wearing a smile so big that you could see all of his teeth.

"It's time," he said. "And you won't believe how beautiful Cora looks."

He led us back down and out of the castle to an open area filled with men, women, and children laughing and dancing to music played by a group of guards and maidens. They were banging their hands on bongos and playing on instruments that I've never seen before. When Cyrus, Fin, Prince Dakota, and I arrived, everyone began to clap and cheer. Prine Dakota led us over to a large pavilion with a long table that was occupied by the tribe's royal family.

"Oliver!" Someone called behind me. I turned back to see Harper and Racheal dancing in the crowd. They both bolted over to me and Harper embraced me. Their hair was tied into braids with strands of silk twirled in, which glimmered from the light of the lamps above our heads.

"You guys look great!" I yelled over the music.

"Thanks!" Harper said, her face turning red as she let go of me.

"Where's Cora?" Fin asked, looking at me with a grin.

"She said she needed a minute to get ready," Racheal answered. "Why?"

"Oh no reason."

Harper lifted an eyebrow before rolling her eyes at Fin and I. Then, Chief Ansel stood up, and everyone went quiet as he began to speak.

"Welcome, everyone! For over five hundred years, our people have been waiting for the descendant of Delphi and her protectors to request our help to defeat the terrible entity that wants to destroy our world, Malice. And now that you are here, we can begin our preparations to help you stop Malice once and for all!" Everyone cheered before Chief Ansel waved for silence. "But first, Oliver Johnson, please step forward."

I looked at Cyrus, Fin, Harper, and Racheal as they nodded in a reassuring way. They pushed me forward, and I walked up the stairs to stand before the chief.

"Where's Princess Cora?" Chief Ansel whispered, his eyes darting around the place in search of her.

"Still getting ready apparently," I whispered back. He nodded and cleared his throat before continuing.

"Oliver Johnson, you have been chosen by the goddess Delphi and Princess Cora to carry the Staff of Light. This staff has been passed down to the one best suited for this perilous journey to aid the descendant of Delphi. As chief of the Tribe, I present you with the Staff. Guards!"

Two guards walked up carrying a long wooden box engraved with a sun and words that spiraled around it. When they opened it, Chief Ansel pulled out a seven foot long golden staff with a large hallowed sun mounted at the top. A long, skinny dragon spiraled its way from the bottom of the staff to the sun top, creating what seemed to be the handle.

"Please, take this, fully knowing how much responsibility is now in your hands." Chief Ansel handed me the staff and a warm but powerful feeling began to spread its way across my body the moment I held it. "May Delphi keep you, the princess, and your friends safe," he prayed. "And now, let us begin our celebration by-" A flash of light illuminated the world around us as a terrible scream pierced the air like a gunshot.

"Racheal!" I whipped around to see Harper, Cyrus, and Fin kneeling down next to Racheal, who lay flat on her back, writhing in pain. Blood was all over her hands and right leg... Which had a black dagger with magenta cracks along its blade lodged into her thigh.

CHAPTER 15

——— ❖ ———

CORA - THE BATTLE OF THE RISING SUN

When Princess Lara, Princess June, Racheal, Harper, and I entered the guest room, I almost wanted to laugh, but not in a bad way!

The room looked almost identical to my room from when I was a kid. It was a large, open room with a chandelier hanging from the ceiling. Two glass doors led out to a balcony with a tall guard rail. A king size bed with a dark wood frame and gold silk sheets was pushed up against the right wall of the room while a huge dresser and vanity were on the left wall. In the center of the room was a mannequin wearing a beautiful emerald green dress that reached the mannequin's knees. It had a golden waist belt and the forearm part of the sleeves were cut off and replaced with gold vambraces.

"This is beautiful," Harper said, wistfully.

"Who is it for?" I asked Princess Lara.

"For you, Princess Cora," she said, pointing up at me. Harper and Racheal looked at each other with their mouths open in shock.

"Cora?" Racheal said, looking at me.

"But why?" Harper asked, sounding jealous.

"This was an outfit that has been repeatedly crafted over and over again for Delphi's first born daughter of every generation. Daddy says that when you wear it, you become closer to Delphi and her spiritual form than ever before." I walked up to the mannequin and took off the outfit, surprised by how light and soft it was. "Go on!" Princess Lara said, smiling. "Try it on."

"We won't look," Racheal promised as they turned around. I took off my torn up five hundred year old outfit and tried on the new one.

It fit perfectly like a glove. The dress made my hips more noticeable and my waist looked skinny. When Harper, Princess Lara, Princess June, and Racheal turned around, they gave an abundance of squeals, cries of delight, and began to check out every inch of the fabric. Even Harper's jealousy seemed to melt away.

After that, Princess Lara found some silver and gold ribbons and we braided them into each other's hair for over a half an hour before Prince Dakota entered the room. When he saw me, his jaw dropped and his eyes took in every inch of me.

"Why, if someone had just told me that the beautiful sun had transformed into a human in this very room, I would've believed that they were talking about you, Cora."

"Awwww," the girls sighed.

"Thanks," I said, trying not to blush. "But everyone looks amazing." Prince Dakota nodded, his face turning more red by the second. Then he shook his head and cleared his throat.

"Father requests all of your presences downstairs."

"Of course!" Princess Lara said, running up and grabbing her brother's hand. "Come on, guys!"

"I'll meet you down there," I said. Princess Lara turned to look back at me.

"Why?" She asked.

"I need to fix my hair. It feels too tight," I lied. "Don't worry, I'll catch up."

"Alright. We'll meet you down there." One by one they all left. Alone in the room, I closed the door behind them. I took a deep breath and walked over to the doors that led to the balcony. I opened them and stepped out into the open air and looked down at the crowd of dancing people below me. I could see the tiny figures of Oliver, Harper, Racheal, Cyrus, and Fin all talking together near a pavilion in front of everyone. Then, I heard a knock on the door and went back inside.

"Come in!" I called. The doors opened as Haki entered, looking very serious.

"What is it, Haki?" I asked. "Is something wrong?"

"Yes," he said. "Malice is here."

My blood turned to ice. "What? How?"

"Malice is able to influence others by reaching into people's minds and controlling them without you sensing it. I saw him use it on a guard down on the second floor! His plan is to kill you, your friends, and the Chief."

"We have to warn them!" I declared.

"No!" Haki yelled. For a moment, his eyes seemed to dilate and turn magenta like Oliver's had when he was possessed.

"Why not, Haki?" I asked, trying to stay calm.

"Because we don't want to cause a panic in the Tribe! I need to get you somewhere safe." He held out his hand, but I didn't take it. "Princess, we don't have time."

"No." Haki looked at me, frustrated.

"Your highness, I'm trying to save your life. Please come with me."

"I will not, Haki," I said. That pushed him over the edge. His eyes turned to fire, flickering in their sockets. His face contorted into an evil grin as a long scythe formed in his hands, glowing a faint purple in the chandelier light. Haki swung his scythe high into the air, and it hit the ground with a loud thud, missing me by only a few inches. He swung again, and I sent a jet of light at him, smacking Haki in the face. He roared in agony.

"Foolish little girl!" He cried, his voice sounding as if three of him were talking at once. "Malice will destroy you!"

"Why are you doing this, Haki?"

"Because I'm tired of following the ways of the tribe. Our chief is simple minded and weak. Malice, however, is strong and won't let anyone stand in his way, even you." Haki summoned a black dagger with magenta cracks on the blade and threw it as hard as he could at me. It missed but tore through my dress as it crashed out of the window and out into the cave. Haki let out a terrifying laugh that made the hair on my arms stand on end. *Ugh, I can never catch a break.* I rushed Haki and disarmed him, sending his scythe clattering to the ground as I pinned him against the wall. I willed my power to try to stop Malice from controlling Haki, but he just kept laughing.

"It's no use," he jeered. "By the time you can stop me, the Tribe of the Rising Sun will fall, and Malice will have the advantage in the coming war!" He continued to laugh, and my anger exploded from me. In a flash of light that emanated from me, I felt Haki's body go limp, and I let him fall to the ground with a thud. He was still breathing, so that was good. I left him there and ran out of the room. When I opened the doors, the two guards at the entrance stood there, looking at me in horror.

"Princess Cora," one of the guards said. "What..?"

"Don't let Haki leave," I ordered. "He's under the influence of Malice." The two guards nodded and readied their spears. I ran down multiple flights of stairs before I heard two loud screams of terror from upstairs.

Haki must have escaped.

After at least five minutes of running, I stopped to catch my breath. I forgot the way out and took a wrong turn! I looked around, trying to figure out which direction I needed to go when I heard footsteps, maybe people, walking towards me. I dove behind a bunch of barrels and went quiet, trying not to make a sound.

"Cora..." Haki's voice called. "I know you're here. Come out! Let's have a chat."

I didn't say anything.

"No?" Haki asked, sounding disappointed. "Then I guess we're going to have to do this the hard way." I leapt out of my hiding place to see Haki and a group of possessed guards standing ten feet away from me. I bolted away from them and back up the stairs. "After her!" Haki screamed. It was the chase of the millennia. I dodged flying weapons, flew around corners, and ran in every direction I could. But no matter what I did, Haki and his men were always behind me. After what seemed like forever, my luck had finally run out. I ran up one more flight of stairs and burst out of a door to what seemed to be the end of the world. I stopped in my tracks and looked down from the highest point of the castle to see nothing but chaos. Below me, I could make out hundreds of tiny people fighting for their lives against undead warriors. Bodies were scattered on the ground like broken dolls as screams and war cries came from below. There was a loud clang, and I looked at the center of the battle to see a figure carrying a glowing golden staff against a shadowy figure. It must be Oliver! He was fighting Malice with the Staff of Light.

"Well, well, well." I whipped around to see the entrance I had just passed. Haki and his men were now standing there. Haki's expression was triumphant now that he knew there was nowhere I could run.

"Haki," I said, trying not to panic. "Listen to me..."

"No," Haki interrupted. "You listen to me." The air seemed to grow cold around me. "You have lost. Malice has won. Now, you must obey him. So give up now or die trying to defend yourself." As he spoke, an idea began to form in my head. A stupid and totally dumb plan, but a plan that could be my only chance to get to Oliver and my friends to help them.

"I'm going to give you to the count of three to surrender before my men cut off your limbs and feed them to the undead warriors," Haki sneered. "One... Two..."

"Three!" I finished. Before any of them could react, I turned and dove off the tower ledge, rocketing down to the battle below. I closed my eyes and began to pray.

Delphi, I prayed. *Help me. Please help me!*

There was a flash of brilliant gold and green light, and I felt arms wrap around me in a warm embrace before my brain became fuzzy as I passed out in the air.

CHAPTER 16

——— ✦ ———

OLIVER - A MESSAGE FROM DELPHI

Before Harper, Racheal, Cyrus, Fin, I, or anyone could do anything, the ground below us quaked as rotting hands shot out from the ground. Women and children screamed in terror. People either ran or were pulled down into the ground by the undead. At the entrance of the tribe, the rock wall exploded with a loud KAHBOOM! As I watched, I saw the glowing figure of Malice leading an army of hundreds, and I mean hundreds, of undead warriors. Each was wearing obsidian armor and carrying all sorts of varying weapons.

"Guards!" Chief Ansel yelled over the chaos. "Protect our people! Everyone inside the castle!"

The crowd broke into two groups: the women and children ran into the castle while all of the men surged forward to meet Malice's army in battle. Somehow, every single one of them had been able to grab something to use as a weapon. One man was carrying a long tiki torch and using it as a bow staff. Another was using a set of bongos and banging the undead warriors on their heads.

"We gotta get Racheal out of here!" I heard Harper yell over the chaos.

"Take her into the castle!" Prince Dakota shouted. Together, Prince Dakota, Harper, Cyrus, and Fin dragged Racheal, who was now moaning in pain, into the castle and propped her up against a wall. I closed the giant door behind us and came over to check on Racheal. Blood was splattered all over the blade of the dagger and slowly seeping into her jeans. Harper reached over to try and pull it out, but she yelped and lept back as purple electricity zapped her fingertips.

"Great," Harper said, her voice sounding as if she was on the verge of tears. "How are we going to get it out of her?" Footsteps echoed through the hallway as Princess Lara, Princess June, and Chieftess Neenah came over to us and knelt down to help Racheal.

Princess Lara gasped in horror, and Cheiftess Neenah covered Lara's eyes though she had already seen what had happened, Lara began to wail and cry.

"Have you tried to pull it out?" Princess June asked.

"Yes," I said. "But it zapped Harper the moment her hand got within six inches of it." Cheiftess Neenah bit her lip as she looked down at Racheal, who was now laying there unconscious on the floor.

"If only Cora were here," Cyrus said. "She probably could've healed Racheal in two seconds!"

"June, sweetie," Chieftess Neenah addressed her eldest daughter. "Take Lara and go find the healer. Oliver..." I looked into her gray eyes, and I could see she looked uncomfortable talking to me. "You must go join the battle."

"What!?! But I don't know how to fight!"

"With that staff you do," the chieftess said, pointing at the staff I held in my hands. "That staff holds the power of Delphi inside it. Whoever is worthy enough to wield it also possesses her powers and Delphi's ability to fight." I looked down at the Staff of Light, astonished how so much power could be in this skinny golden stick.

"Go, Oliver," Cyrus said, gesturing for me to move.

"We'll stay here with Racheal," Fin said, nodding reassuringly. However, his eyes gave it away that he was worried. I nodded, looking one last time at Racheal before getting up, opening the entrance door and walking out into the raging battle outside.

"You've got this, Oliver!" Harper hollered.

When I got outside, the clanging and clattering of swords and battle cries met my ears. I took a deep breath and clenched my fists on the staff. I felt it vibrate beneath my fingertips as it glowed a faint gold. A warm feeling began to spread through my body and I began to feel confident. So, I ran into the battle. As I fought, I went on autopilot. For some reason, my brain knew what I was doing, but I wasn't the one who was controlling my body. I dodged, rolled, stabbed, parried, and rammed into the undead warriors. The power of the staff seemed to guide me through battle as I decimated every enemy in sight. At one point, I had to try not to vomit as I stepped over the bodies of a couple guards, all of whom were disintegrating as a black and magenta goo oozed its way around them.

Finally, I must have gotten Malice's attention because I could feel his terrible power coming closer as his shadowy figure came towards me. When he saw me, he charged, swinging two large katanas in the air. I rolled to the side and lunged, clanging into his armor. As we continued to fight, the world seemed to tear itself apart as the forces of good and evil fought, each trying to dominate the other.

"Foolish boy, you think you can stop me with that puny staff? Ha! You're wrong." Malice slashed downward, and I blocked, holding him at a stand still.

"For the record..." I said, smiling. "You say 'foolish' a lot. Is that like your catchphrase or something?" Malice growled in annoyance before something above us caught his eye.

"Hey, Oliver," Malice sneered at me. "Looks like your princess is about to take the leap of faith."

"What?" I turned my head to look up and see Cora standing on the ledge of the highest tower of the castle. "Cora?"

Before I could stop him, Malice slashed one sword at me and sliced my arm. Pain shot through my body, and, with the force of a thousand bulls, Malice hit me with the butt of his other sword and sent me flying twenty... no... thirty feet into the air. The staff created a cushion beneath me to break my fall, but it was still a hard landing. I looked back up and kept my eyes on Cora, not caring what Malice was doing.

"Cora!" I called up to her. But I faltered and watched in terror as Cora turned on the spot and jumped off the castle tower, plummeting to the ground. "NO!" I screamed. Out of the corner of my eye, I saw Malice racing toward me with a murderous expression. I didn't even get up to defend myself. Instead, I braced myself for the fatal blow of his katanas.

A flash of golden and green light blinded me, and I shielded my eyes. I heard Malice scream in anguish while every single undead warrior turned to ash the moment the light shone upon them. Something large flew over my head, making my hair ruffle from the slight breeze. I dared to look up and gasped in astonishment to see Cora flying above our heads. A faint green outline of dragon wings had appeared on her back, flapping to keep her in the air. She circled around Malice and me. She then landed beside me and helped me up. When I looked closer at her, I saw that instead of Cora's normal blue or gold eye color, her eyes were neon green. The staff of light began to vibrate again and pull in the direction of Cora. She turned away from me and faced Malice, her teeth gritted.

"Malice," Cora growled. Behind her voice, I could make out two other voices. One sounded more mature and woman-like: kind of like a mother's voice. The other sounded like the voice of a dragon which made the hair on the back of my neck stand up. That's when it hit me. Those wings and eye color weren't something that Cora could do with her normal powers. It was as if someone else was influencing her, someone more powerful.

"Delphi," Malice hissed, "it's been a long time."

"Leave, Malice. You are not welcome here."

"But I own the shadows," he sneered, smiling at her. "Caves are like a second home to me. Especially after you put us down in that chasm for so long." Cora, I mean, Delphi, clenched her fists.

"You've done enough damage for today," Delphi said. "So go before I decide to turn you into a grease spot on the ground."

"Oh, Delphi," Malice laughed. "We both know that you won't do such a thing. That's Cora's job in the end. Isn't it? The prophecy says she is the one destined to destroy me once and for all." Before Delphi could respond, Malice vanished in a cloud of black smoke. I covered my mouth as I coughed and gagged from the smoke's smell, which was like rotting flesh and brussel sprouts.

"Oliver," Delphi said. I turned to face her. It was so hard to not think that she was Cora, despite Delphi controlling Cora's body. However, I couldn't help but feel a little awkward. "Take Racheal, Cora, and your friends to the Temple of the Sun. It's on the Island of Shadows. There, Racheal will be able to heal, and Cora can complete the last thing she needs before her final fight with Malice." Delphi waved her hand and a pile of paper scrolls, maps, and charts appeared at my feet. "These will help you find the location of the temple." I nodded and knelt down to start gathering the papers.

"Oliver, one more thing." I got back up and looked at Delphi. She shifted uncomfortably. "It wasn't I who chose you to carry the Staff of Light. Cora did. She saw something in you that made her know she could trust you no matter what. All I ask is that you make sure to keep Cora safe."

"I will. I promise," I said confidently. Though in the back of my mind, the words of Cora's prophecy echoed in my head. "*And they shall lose her to worse than death...*"

Delphi smiled at me. "I understand now why she chose you. You're just like someone she knew a very, very long time ago." Then, she cleared her throat. "I shall go and so should you. I suggest you leave in the morning and head to the temple. Hopefully, you can get there without any problems. Goodbye, Oliver." Then, the faint outline of dragon wings and Cora's green eyes faded away, and I caught Cora as she collapsed.

Chapter 17

Cora - The Voyage

After Oliver explained what had happened when I had passed out, we arrested Haki and helped the Tribe treat the injured soldiers. The following morning we took a limo to take a boat to the island. The reason why we had to take a limo was because of how much space we needed for Racheal and the floating platform she was on. Fin suggested that we should rent a hearse, but we thought that was creepy and not the right time. As we boarded the boat, two of the Tribe's appointed guards took Rachael's unconscious body to the lower deck while Oliver, Fin, Cyrus, Harper, and I went into the tiny lounge to try and find the location of the temple in the pile of scrolls that Delphi handed to Oliver before we left. For the next few hours, we translated and read every single word, desperately trying to find anything. But in the end, our research bore no fruit.

I was kneeling on the ship floor, reading a small bit of writing on the bottom of a scroll when Fin sighed and dropped his chart next to me.

"That was the last one," he muttered.

"We have to keep looking," I said. "We can't just give up."

"She's right," Harper said, rolling up the scroll she was looking at.

"But we've looked everywhere. There's nothing that specifically says where to go!" We were silent for a moment before Cyrus, whose face was turning red, tore his scroll in two and stood up.

"This is your fault Cora!"

"What?" I said, taken aback. I stood up, and Cyrus got aggressively in my face.

"If it weren't for you, we would've never gotten into this mess; we'd be safe right now, and Racheal..." He cleared his throat. "She wouldn't have a magical dagger lodged in her thigh and be on her deathbed!"

"Cyrus, you don't mean that!" Harper argued, placing a hand on Cyrus' shoulder. He shrugged it off.

"Yes, I do!" He shouted. "We wouldn't be here if Cora would've been able to fulfill her prophecy! You're a failure, Cora!" By then, I began to feel hot tears trickling down my cheek. In the back of my mind, I remembered something just like this that happened to me when I was a little girl...

Except that was even more unpleasant.

"Let's go..." Oliver whispered in my ear while placing a hand on my shoulder. Suddenly, anger and fear flared up inside me. My mind was sent back into an old memory of someone I loved. A tall, muscular figure with a golden crown loomed high above my head.

"A descendant of Delphi, my own daughter even, is a failure!" The man raised his giant hand high into the air, a ring glinting in the torch-light. "I will make you understand the importance of your mission, Cora..." His hand swung down quickly, and I didn't have time to defend myself...

"Don't hit me!" I shrieked. An energy blast shot through me, and Oliver, Harper, Fin, and Cyrus were hit square in the stomach, being forced to take a few steps back.

"Woah... Cora..?" But I ran out of the lounge to the main deck.

*** ***

Oliver found me a few minutes later, leaning against the rail of the ship with tears silently streaming down my face. He walked over and stood next to me but kept his distance.

"Cora, what just happened? I've never seen you do that before." I sniffed while wiping tears from my eyes. I could still feel fear stirring inside me like butterflies.

"A long time ago," I began. "When I was a young girl, I came down to the throne room to tell my father once again that I was still not able to summon my power. When I arrived and told my father what had happened, he became agitated and vile. He yelled at me. He told me that I was a failure and how I would be the reason for this world's destruction. He claimed I was running out of time... and that's when he hit me." I stopped, choking back another wave of tears.

"Your father hit you?" Oliver asked, shocked. I nodded.

"He was wearing one of his jeweled rings that night, so I even have a scar to prove it." I pulled back a lock of hair to show Oliver a small scar near my temple.

"Did you tell anyone?"

"No," I said, shaking my head. "Women and girls were looked down upon by men. Sure, the guards and everyone in the city respected me and my family because of our royal blood, but my father was the king and in charge of everyone. He was allowed to do whatever he wanted, and no one could stop him."

"That's terrible, so that's why you freaked out?"

"It felt like I went back in time and now with Racheal almost..." My voice cracked as I choked up. Oliver wrapped his arm around me, pulled me close, and embraced me in a hug. I didn't pull away. Instead, I buried my face into his chest and sobbed. Slowly, my fear inside me ebbed away to transform into something new and unusual.

"Guys! Oh, sorry." Oliver let go of me, and we both looked to see Fin standing about twenty feet away.

"What do you want, Fin?" Oliver asked.

"Oh! We think we found something, but we need Cora to translate."

"We'll be there in a minute," Oliver replied. Fin smiled and rolled his eyes. He turned away and walked out of sight.

"Come on, Oliver. Let's go help them." I started to walk away, but Oliver's hand grabbed mine.

"Cora, there's something I need to tell you."

"Can it wait?" I asked. "Racheal's life is on the line!" Oliver paused, his mouth open as if to speak.

"Uhhhh..." He swallowed. "Yeah, it can wait." I smiled at him and he smiled back. However, I could tell that something was bothering him. We walked away from the ship's rail and back to the lounge.

When we got back, Cyrus immediately apologized for his actions and begged me to forgive him. I forgave him, and he gave me something called a "fist bump", whatever that means. That's when Harper handed me a scroll that showed an old drawing of a mountain with a sun rising in the top left corner. I looked at it, completely confused.

"So, why do you want me to look at this?" I asked Harper. "It's just a drawing."

"Because we found something on this scroll that we think only you'll know. Just take a closer look at the sun." I pulled the scroll closer to my face, and I realized there was a different language written inside the drawing of the sun.

"Do you know what language it is?" Racheal asked me.

"It's the language of Delphi."

"Huh?"

"It was one of the first languages ever created in the world."

"Wait," Oiver said. "Was that the weird language that we heard you speaking in with that creature at the school?" I nodded.

"Do you know what it says?" Cyrus asked. I placed a finger on the letters, and they began to glow gold as the writing changed to English. That's when I began to speak:

"To the one who holds the power of the sun,

For then the battle has now truly begun.

At the last light of day,

The sun will bend your way.

Then cast the light into the dragon's eye,

And you shall see the Temple rise.

Only when mortal and immortal combine,

will then lead to a path of powers divine."

"Ok," Cyrus began. "That makes no sense."

"Maybe it's a riddle?" Harper said, her eyebrows furrowed.

"No," Oliver said. "It's a message written in verse!"

"Isn't that something that Shakespeare wrote for some of his plays?" Racheal asked.

"I think so." Oliver answered.

"Who's Shakespeare?" I asked.

"You don't know Shakespeare!?!" Fin asked, exasperated. "He's..."

"Guys!" Oliver, interjected. "We're getting off topic! We need to figure this out."

"Well," I said. "We already knew we needed to go to the Island of Shadows. That's one thing."

"Then let's continue our course to the island so we at least get there,' Oliver said.

"Agreed," I turned to Harper. "Please inform the captain that we are still continuing to the original destination."

"On it." Harper ran out of the room, and we looked at each other, our brains flooded with excitement and anticipation. This may be our one best and only shot to save Racheal!

That's when I heard something that made my hair stand on end.

CHAPTER 18

— · —

OLIVER - THE ISLAND OF SHADOWS

The moment Cora's face fell, I knew something was about to happen. She yelled, "Bomb!" We all covered our heads as the entire boat exploded with a loud: BOOM! We were shot into the sky then crashed into the sea. Before I blacked out, I saw a pale hand gently grab mine, pulling me back up toward the light.

When I woke up, Cora was shaking my shoulder violently, repeatedly saying my name. I could feel that my clothes were sopping wet and my hands were submerged in dry sand. I also felt a shooting pain in my leg. I opened my eyes to see an open blue sky above me and Cora's face inches from mine. I tried to sit up, but Cora slowly lowered me back down.

"No, stay still." She placed a hand on my chest, and a warm feeling spread through my body. The pain in my leg vanished, and I sighed in relief.

"Where is everyone?" I asked, my voice sounding faint.

"Cyrus and Fin went to find wood to start a fire."

"What about Harper and the others?"

Cora lowered her head in despair, and I remembered that they weren't with us when the boat exploded. But, they could've survived the crash... Right?

"Could it be possible they were stranded on the other side of the island?" I asked, hopefully.

"Yes, I was just about to see if I could find them."

"Shouldn't we just wait until morning?"

"By then it might be too late to save Racheal if she's still alive. We're racing against the clock."

"You go," I said.

She nodded in agreement. "I'll try to get back before it gets too dark," Cora said, confidently. "Besides, Cyrus and Fin should be back any minute." She ran off into the trees and disappeared into the shadows. The moment she left, I could feel my survival instincts kicking in. I listened to the slightest movements in the bushes and flinched at every breeze that blew past me. About an hour later, the stars started to appear in the sky and I started to get a little worried. *Cyrus, Fin, and Cora should've been back by now, right?*

"Maybe I should find them?" I muttered to myself.

"Unfortunately, you won't be able to look for them," a voice said. I turned to see a boy about my age, but he wasn't exactly a boy. He had red skin, black hair that was styled into a mohawk. He wore nothing but a bone necklace made of different skulls and a golden belt, which was connected to a red swirling tornado that replaced his legs.

"Who are you?" I asked.

"Pardon my manners," the boy said. "My name is Daemon. I am known as a djinn."

"Aren't djinn's supposed to be like evil genies or something? And why can't I go looking for my friends?"

"Oh! Well, I found your friends for you!" Daemon flicked his hand, and Harper, Racheal, Cyrus, Fin, Cora, the boat driver, and the guards appeared: tied together with red chains, and black cloths were shoved into their mouths. All of them were unconscious. I gasped in shock.

"Guys!" I got up, but Daemon snapped his fingers, and I froze, unable to move a muscle.

"What do you want with them?" I asked, my teeth clenched.

"Well, one of them is very powerful. More powerful than me perhaps." He floated Cora's unconscious body toward him. Cora's hair seemed to flow around her as her skin glowed in the starlight. "She is beautiful, isn't she? It's as if the most majestic sunrise became a human girl! I'm sure she'll make a wonderful ally. She just needs a little... persuasion." He brushed his hand against her face, and I felt my blood begin to boil with anger.

"Don't touch her!" I hissed.

"Oh! Protective, are we? How touching," he laughed, making my hair stand on end. He snapped his fingers again, and everything turned black around me as I passed out. By the time I woke up, I was tied up in a chair in a dining room with windows all around us. I looked to my right, and I saw Cora next to me, her head lolled to one side, and her hands and feet were bound in black chains that glowed red.

"Cora, wake up! Wake up!" Her eyes opened, and she looked around, taking in her surroundings.

"Oliver? What's going on?"

"We've been taken by a djinn."

"Wait, what?"

Daemon appeared in front of us along with a table covered in an arrangement of sweets, a variety of meat delicacies, mashed potatoes, and a tower of rainbow colored fruit. The smell was overpowering. My mouth began to water, and my eyes grew wide. "Are you two hungry?" he asked, smiling. I almost said yes, but Cora kicked me in the shin, and I snapped out of it.

"I don't eat food that belongs to a thing that keeps me hostage," Cora said, sounding extremely hostile.

"Well, that's too bad. I was hoping you would like to try the chicken marsala. No? Okay then..." Daemon waved his hand and the food disappeared in a puff of red smoke.

"What do you want with us anyway?" Cora asked, her teeth clenched.

"Well, I've been waiting for someone like you, Cora. Your powers are unlike any I've seen."

"Your point?" She asked, sounding annoyed.

"All I ask of you is to join me. Together, we could rule the world."

"No, thanks," Cora answered.

"What?" Demon said, confused. "But you and I together... well, we would be impossible to defeat!"

"Still, no," Cora said, calmly.

"Come on..." He tried to stroke her cheek, but she gnashed her teeth at him. He glided back.

"So, you don't want to help me then." He floated away until he was next to one of the glass windows. "Well, I guess I'll have to take drastic measures now. Oh well." He waved his hand and outside the window, Cyrus, Fin, Harper, the guards, the boat driver, and Racheal appeared, tied together, floating in mid air about five hundred feet in the sky. Even from here, we could hear their loud, piercing screams.

"Let them go!" Cora said.

"It's not that simple, Cora. I can let them go. But only for a small price."

"Like what?" Cora asked, her voice full of rage.

"Well, if you don't want to help me..."

"You need my power..." Cora finished, her face breaking into realization.

Daemon smiled. "I see that we are on the same page."

"Why can't you just take my power?" Cora asked, exasperated. "Surely, you, all powerful, don't need me to give it to you."

"Oh, Cora, you poor naive girl." Daemon's expression looked almost pitiful. Just him looking at her seemed to make me wanna tear him to pieces. "You haven't even scratched the surface of your powers, and if my powers combine with yours, no one could stop me!" He laughed at the mere thought of it.

"I won't let you get away with this!" Cora snapped. "My power isn't for taking."

"Oh, well. That's fine." He turned to watch the others screaming far away. "You just might want to change your mind before your friends go skydiving."

CHAPTER 19

———— ❦ ————

CORA - FORGOTTEN MEMORIES

Oliver and I struggled to break free of the chains. I looked down and saw my hands were beginning to turn dry and red where the djinni's chains came in contact with my skin. Oliver nudged me, as if telling me to stop fighting, but I ignored it, looking up at Daemon.

"Please! Let Oliver and others go! They have nothing to do with this!"

"But they're your motivation, Cora," Daemon crooned. "How would you make a quick decision without me putting you under pressure? Tut tut tut... Time is precious."

He turned to look outside, and we still could hear Cyrus, Fin, Harper, and the others screaming for help. I struggled at the chains for a few seconds as my brain grew desperate. Suddenly, an idea came into my head. I bowed my head as if in defeat. My hair covered my face so that none of them could see my expression.

"Fine," I muttered. "What do you want me to do?"

"What! Cora, don't do this. We can find another way..."

"Silence!" Daemon ordered. He swiped his hand in the air, and Oliver went silent. "You must wish to give me your power," Daemon whispered, sending chills down my spine like raindrops on a leaf, slowly sliding down to the tips of my toes.

"And if I do it," I said, looking up at him, "will you let them go?"

"Of course!"

I looked out the window at where Harper, Fin, Cyrus, and the others were. Out of the corner of my eye, I saw Oliver looking at me closely. He must have realized that there weren't any tears in my eyes because his expression changed slightly. Finally, I spoke.

"Fine. I'll do it, but let them go first." Daemon stood there, his eyebrows were furrowed in thought.

"Deal." Daemon waved his hand, and Racheal, Cyrus, Fin, and the others disappeared in a cloud of dust. His expression changed as he smiled.

"I kept my side of the bargain. Now you must, too."

"Fine. I wish..."

I stayed silent for a moment, biting my lip. Oliver stared at me in disbelief. *Oh Delphi, please let this plan work.*

"I wish we could go back to before we met you!" I said, looking up at him.

The world around us spun, and in a flash of red light, we appeared back in time. We were on a shingled rooftop of a huge mansion. Looking down, we could see six figures below. The sun was cascading light down so that a little pond on the left glittered up at us. Looking closer at the figures, I could see a younger version of myself, maybe eight or nine years old. My hair was tied back into a ponytail, and I was wearing a green, silk shirt, blue jeans, and golden colored shoes. My face was blank, and my posture made me look like a statue. Daemon did a full three-sixty to take in the entire view of the scenery.

"Ahh, now what do we have here?"

Oliver looked at me, trying to catch my eye, but I continued to stare blankly at my younger self and the other figures below. I watched two teenagers, boys that were about my age, battling, sword against bow and arrow. One shot a volley of arrows at the other, but he dodged them, stepped to the side of the boy with the arrows, turned him over, and slammed the boy onto the ground face first, knocking the wind out on him. The boy who was still standing roared with laughter at defeating his opponent.

"I win again!" He hollered in delight.

"No fair! You were in my blind spot! The sun was in my eyes!"

"Yeah, right!"

The two boys laughed together, and the boy standing helped the other off the ground.

"Who are those two?" Oliver whispered to me.

"That's Kane," I muttered, pointing to the one with the arrows. "And that's Nick." I pointed to the one with the sword. Oliver looked closer at the other three that were off to the side.

"That's you, right?" He points to the younger version of myself below.

"Yes, that's me," I said, nodding.

"And the other two?"

"The girl's name is Lilly, and the boy is Luke." I again pointed to the two people that stood next to the younger me. Lilly wore a chest guard and carried a golden sword that had carvings of leaves and flowers up and down the handle. Out of the corner of my eye, I saw someone move. I turned and saw that Luke was walking up next to Nick and Kane, who were still laughing together, but when Nick and Kane saw him, they stopped.

"Even if Nick was in your blind spot Kane, you should always be aware of the possibility of being attacked from that angle," Luke said, hardening his gaze. "It will be used against you!"

"It's just a training exercise, Luke," Nick remarked, rolling his eyes. "It's not like it's the real deal."

"Then you should treat it like the 'real deal!'" Luke snapped.

Nick and Luke glared at each other for a moment, but then Luke turned to look at Lilly and Cora.

"Positions." He called over to them. Lilly and Cora looked at each other. Lilly put a hand on the young Cora's shoulder and nodded at

Luke. Kane and Nick walked to the edge of the grass as Lilly and Cora walked forward until they were in the center of the yard.

"Once more! Cora and Lilly. Ready?" Lilly and Cora both looked at each other. The young Cora's expression was blank, but Lily's expression was content and excited.

"Go!"

With a swish and swirling of swords, Lilly and Cora flew right at each other. Within a split second, Lilly disarmed Cora and pinned her to the ground. Even from above, I could see two scarlet gashes on Cora's cheek and hand.

"Oh my gosh! Cora, are you ok?" Lilly helped Cora up and examined her hand and face. "I didn't mean to hurt you."

Cora looked at her in confusion. "What do you mean?"

"Look at your hand and your face. Don't you feel the stinging?" Cora looked at her hand and felt her face as blood trickled down her cheek.

"I guess not. I didn't even notice..." Daemon had a slightly shocked expression on his face. He turned and looked at Cora.

"Why did you wish to see this?" Daemon asked, curiosity in his voice.

"I didn't... You did. You picked a part of my memory that you guessed would make me want to leave. You chose one that you thought made me look weak." I looked at him and smiled. "But it doesn't. That fight was a great learning experience for me. Therefore, it doesn't make me sad." Daemon stood there, stunned for a moment. Then, his face turned red, his expression full of hatred and fury.

"How... dare you! I am the all powerful djinn!"

"You want my next wish, Daemon? Well here it is, I wish to go back."

Another flash of light, and we appeared in a master bedroom. Looking around, I saw walls that were a pale sun color, a bed with covers that were made of golden silk woven together, books that were stacked as far as the eye can see, and a book that lay on the bed with a stuffed teddy bear next to it. There was also a huge window with golden drapes that were hung to the side of the window

"Where are we?" Daemon looked around and floated over to the window.

"My home," I said. I looked down at my hands which were still chained up, but the djinn's chains had become just normal chains. Daemon had not noticed yet. In one swift movement, my hands glowed brightly, and the chains turned to dust. I slashed my hand through the air, and Daemon went flying back. He hit the wall and fell to the ground, disoriented and dazed. I waved my hand and glowing golden chains cuffed Daemon's hands. I waved my hand again, and the chains on Oliver's wrists disappeared. I ran over to where Oliver and Daemon were, stopping to look down at Daemon.

"Oh, I forgot to mention this before I made my wish." I walked over to a drawer, opened it, found a sock, turned around, came back, and stuffed it in Daemon's mouth so he couldn't say anything. "Djinn magic doesn't work on others in the castle unless requested by the king."

Daemon struggled and tried to escape. He roared in frustration, but the sound was muffled by the sock. I raised my hand to the sky, and Daemon was lifted into the air. His body went limp like a puppet being dangled from its strings. The only thing that wasn't limp was his head. He glared at me, his expression full of hatred.

"I knew you were going to try and break me again. Well, that's not going to work. I'm just one step ahead of..." Suddenly, I stopped. We stood there, silent, as we heard a soft voice whispered from out in the hallway:

"Come out, come out wherever you are."

Daemon smiled, knowing he had finally gotten to me. In one movement, I lowered Daemon onto the ground, flicking my hand to force Oliver under the bed, and I dove behind a pile of books. I looked out from behind the books where it was harder to see me. A woman with long, red hair and green eyes walked in, smiling. She wore a golden dress that flowed out behind her. A golden crown with emeralds was placed on her head. It was my mother.

"I know you're in here," she whispered. I held my breath, trying to not make a sound. My mother walked in a few steps, shuffled a few things around, then walked out. I got up, assuming that it was 'all clear'. Oliver got up, too. I grabbed Daemon by his armor with surprising strength and took the sock out of Daemon's mouth. My heart pounded in my chest. If this was the memory I think it is... Then... No... I did not want to relive that.

"Take us back home!" I whispered, my voice becoming panicky.

"But you are home." Demon said, slyly.

"That's not what I meant."

"Then wish it all to go away. I can send you back."

I bit my lip, thinking. "I'm not falling for that."

"Fine, then watch... Watch as you relive one of your worst memories."

Daemon gestured to the window. I let go of him, turned, and walked to the window. Oliver followed me, and together, we looked down to view one of the most beautiful gardens I'd ever seen. Bushes that were as tall as a crabapple tree were on the outskirts of the garden. Bright, rainbow colored flowers covered the ground, and a winding path cut between the flowers. Two shadows showed where two people were hiding. One was hiding behind a stone statue of a dragon in the center of the garden. The other was behind a row of bushes on the far right side. Immediately, I recognized the girl behind the bushes as a very young version of myself.

"Who is the other girl?" Oliver asked, turning to look at me. I didn't move, all I could do was stare at the scene in horror, knowing what would happen next.

Just then, mother walked out into the garden and peered around bushes. Even inside, a loud giggle fluttered through the air. Mother paused and the laughter died instantly. She turned, walked over to the statue, and plucked a little girl from behind it. The girl had long red hair, steel gray eyes, and she wore a dress that was an emerald green. My heart melted as I immediately recognized the little girl.

"You caught me!" my little sister, Grace, squealed.

"Shh," my mother said, rocking the little girl. She looked around then whispered, "Tell me where she is." Grace pointed to where my younger self was hiding. Mom set Grace down and crept over. She pushed apart the bushes and looked down at my younger self. "Gotcha!"

"No fair! Grace helped you!"

"But either way, you win!" Grace argued.

Grace and my younger self stuck their tongues out at each other then burst into a fit of laughter. A figure slithered toward them. Looking at the entrance of the garden, Oliver's jaw dropped in shock as he saw who the scaly creature was.

It was Deku.

But he didn't look... evil.

Deku looked different. He wore golden armor that glistened in the sunlight, a long sword was strapped to his back, and he was smiling. Mother saw him and smiled back. I felt my fists clench. She looked down at her two daughters.

"That's enough, you two. Now, go play by yourselves for a while." The younger Cora and Grace ran off, chasing each other around the garden.

"Your highnessss," Deku said, bowing.

"What is it?" Mother asked.

"The king is in trouble."

"What?" She looked to see where the two girls were, then looked back at Deku. "How? Where is he?"

"There is a riot outside the castle. They won't let him back inside."

Mother's face fell. "Stay here with the children. I'll go see if I can do anything."

"Yesss, your highnessss."

Mother ran down the path and went inside. Deku stood there for a moment, before his armor changed from gold to dark matter and his expression became malevolent. He slowly slithered over to where Grace and the younger me were playing. They had stopped together at the edge of the garden and had started playing. His shadow loomed over them, and they turned around.

"Deku," My younger self said, looking confused, "What are you doing?"

Deku opened his hand and an orb of dark matter appeared.

"Proving my allegiance, your 'highnesss.'"

He raised the orb over his head when, out of nowhere, Mother came running at him, a golden sword made of sunlight in her hand. She slammed hard into Deku, and he flew high into the air before crashing onto a bunch of flowers. Within a second, Mother had the tip of the sword at Deku's throat. The orb of dark matter still hovered in Deku's open palm.

"It's over, Deku," she said, glaring at him. Deku glanced at the orb in his hand and grinned.

"No," he said, looking back at her. "This is only the beginning."

Deku disappeared in a puff of purple smoke and reappeared at the entrance of the garden. He sent the dark matter orb flying at my younger self's face.

"No!"

Time seemed to slow down as high above, inside the castle, Daemon, Oliver, and I watched as my mother ran towards her eldest daughter. She dove in front of me and got hit straight in the chest with the dark matter orb. She fell onto the ground and lay there, motionless. Deku let out a roar of anger and disappointment before disappearing, leaving the two girls alone. Both Grace and my younger self knelt down next to Mother and started tapping and shaking her, trying to wake her up from a place she could never come back from. Their screams and wails pierced the air like cannon fire.

"Mom? Mom. Please get up! Please! Somebody help!"

"No. No!" Inside the castle, I felt hot tears flood from my eyes as I collapsed onto my knees and covered my ears. Trying to drown out the noise and the feeling of pain. "I wish it all to go away! I wish to go back to the present!" There was another flash of light, and Daemon, Oliver, and I landed in an empty hallway of the castle. My chains I had put on Daemon were gone and I was kneeling on the floor. Daemon looked down at me, his face looked content, but there was a slight sadness in his eyes. Oliver held out his hand and helped me to my feet. When I looked at him, his expression made him look like he had just seen a ghost. I looked around, tears streaming down my face. We were still inside of the castle, but it was night. Above us, I could hear the sound of rain pouring down onto the roof.

"Where... Why are we in the castle?"

"You said you wanted to go back to the present."

"This isn't what I meant..." I said, my voice cracking.

"You must be careful with what you say."

"I don't understand. Daemon, why did you..." Before I could finish, Daemon disappeared. "Daemon!?" My voice echoed down the empty hallway. A door opened nearby, and Oliver pointed to a large cabinet. We both climbed in and closed the door, leaving a crack in it to see who was there. A younger Cora walked out into the hallway and looked around. She wore a white nightgown and was wiping her face clean of tears. She turned and started to walk quietly forward down the hallway when a voice came from the shadows.

"What are you doing out here, Cora?"

"Dad."

A tall, burly, male figure walked down the hallway. He wore long, emerald robes with golden cuffs and edges. A large crown with emerald rubies rested on his head. He had buzzed, brown hair and steel gray eyes. He stopped in front of his daughter and glared down at her.

"Uhhh... I just... wanted to walk around."

"It isn't safe for you to walk around the castle alone. Especially after what happened..." He lifted his head, as if wanting to see the sky, then looked back down. I could see that his eyes were glossy as if he had been crying too.

"Father," my younger self said, her voice shaking. She clenched her fists and looked into her father's eyes. "I am more than capable of walking along the hallways on my own. I don't need anyone to protect me. Deku is gone, and I wish to see Grace. She has been locked up in her room for too long. I can hear her crying at night. She needs to be comforted." Father looked away from her.

"She will get over it. Just as you and I have."

My younger self stared at him. Even though my face looked blank, I remembered how furious I was with my father.

"Cora..." Father brought out a small, wooden musical box that looked miniscule in his huge hand. "Your mother wanted to give this to you for your birthday. But since she is... gone, I wanted to give it to you now." He placed the little music box in my tiny hands.

"But," I stammered, "my birthday isn't until tomorrow."

"I understand that. But tomorrow, Luke and the other protectors will be coming to take you away from the palace to start your training in hand to hand combat."

My younger self looked at my father, dumbfounded. "What!?! But Father!"

"I will not let your mother's death get in the way of you completing our family's legacy."

"But..."

"That is enough, Cora!" He glared at her. "Tomorrow morning you will pack your things and leave." Cora opened her mouth as if she was going to argue.

"Do you understand me!?!

The young Cora paused, closed her mouth, then bowed her head.

"Yes, Father."

"I will walk you back to your room." She walked back to her room with her father. However, before he opened the door, she turned around.

"Father, can I go tell Grace the news? It's only fair."

Father looked down at her, his expression sad. "Fine, but you must return to your room as soon as you are done talking to her."

"Understood."

The younger Cora ran down the hallway and disappeared. Then, Father disappeared as he rounded the corner. When the two weren't in sight, Oliver and I opened the cabinet door and fell out. I got to my feet and looked around.

"Daemon!" I whispered. With a small pop, Daemon appeared next to us.

"Yes?"

"Why are we here? I asked you to take me back to the present."

"Yes, and that's exactly what I did. Didn't you see the little present your father gave to you?" A feeling of ice began creeping its way through my body as I realized what he had done. He twisted my words again!

"Are you telling me... But if you did what I think you did... oh no..."

"Ahh, so you do understand your situation here." Daemon said.

"But you can't just..."

"Oh yes I can." Daemon intervened, grinning slyly at me. "You see, you used all of your wishes, Cora. So, you can't wish for yourself to go back to your friends."

"But I know you won't leave me here. You still need my powers."

"Do I?"

He raised his hand. A sword made of light appeared in his hands; a sword just mine. Instinctively, I raised my hand, but nothing happened.

"But... How?" I slashed my hand through the air, trying to summon a beam of light. but again, nothing happened.

"Tut. Tut. It seems that I have everything that I need. Thank you for 'wishing it all away.'" Daemon let out a mirthless laugh.

"No!"

I lunged at him but he disappeared. My heart was going so fast I thought it was going to explode.

Oliver and I were lost in time, and I had no power to save us now.

CHAPTER 20

OLIVER - THE LOST SONG

I helped Cora get up, and she brushed off her outfit.

"Great. Just great."

"What do we do now?" I asked.

"I don't know."

Cora looked around to see if we were still the only ones there. Then, she turned and ran down the hallway where the younger Cora had gone. I followed after her. Somehow, I just knew where she was going.

"There's a shortcut to the right. Come on!" We turned right and continued to run down the hallway. Cora moved a tapestry which revealed a long, dark passageway that tunneled down into the earth. Torches flickered against the stone walls lining the passage.

"Let's go." We ran down the stairs, up a ladder, and opened a trap door to crawl out beneath a bed. I bumped my head against the wooden frame and winced. Cora clapped her hand over my mouth and put her finger to her lips before pointing up above us. Even though it was very quiet, I could hear faint voices.

"Why does father always send you away? I barely see you." I looked at Cora, and she mouthed, "Grace." I immediately understood that she meant her little sister was sitting on the bed above us.

"You know that I have my role to play in the prophecy." Cora looked at me and pointed at herself to indicate that it was her younger self talking.

"Why can't you just earn your blessing by praying to Delphi? Then father wouldn't send you away, and we could be together." I looked at Cora

"It's not that simple..."

"I always ask Father why can't I take your place for once, but he never answers."

"Grace, it's not something that you can just switch places with a person. It's always been the first born of every generation. You know that." They both were quiet for a moment. The bed squeaked as Grace cuddled closer to the younger Cora. Above us, I heard Grace burst into tears.

"I just wish Mom was here."

"Shhh. I know." Then, young Cora began to sing. It sounded like an angel from heaven singing or a breeze in the wind, soft and quiet.

"You are my sunshine,

my only sunshine.

You make me happy,

when skies are gray.

You'll never know dear,

how much I love you.

Please don't take my sunshine away."

Grace sniffled. "Mommy used to sing that at night. It always helped me fall asleep." The bed squeaked as the younger Cora got off of the bed and helped Grace get tucked in.

"I'm really gonna miss you, Grace."

"Then stay," Grace said. "Stay here, and don't go! I can hide you under the bed. They'll never find you!"

"I have to go. If I don't, our home would be destroyed. You're just too young to-"

"Understand? I know... Just go."

"Grace..."

"Get out of my room, Cora!" Grace snapped, her bed squeaking as she rolled over.

"Ok." The younger Cora turned, and I watched her feet move toward the door. She turned to look back at her sister before leaving the room.

"You're my sister, Grace and I'll always love you. No matter where I am. I'll never forget you." Silence. Then, younger Cora left, and we heard Grace burst into tears, sobbing uncontrollably for what seemed to be at least ten minutes before her sobbing became shallow breaths and then steady, quiet breathing. She had fallen asleep. Then, Cora rolled out from under the bed and stood up surprisingly quietly and quickly. I followed, and we tip-toed across the room, heading toward the door.

"What do we do now?" I whispered to Cora, grabbing her wrist to stop her.

"Find Daemon." She said, turning to look at me. "He couldn't just leave us behind."

"Couldn't he?" I asked. "He's a djinn. He can do anything." I looked at her gaze and realized she wasn't focused on me. "What are you looking at?" I turned around and saw the small music box with gold paint painted around the edges that sat on the bedside table next to Grace's bed. My grip slackened on her wrist, and Cora quietly walked back.

"What are you doing?" My mouth dropped. She picked up the little music box. "Cora, you can't just take something from the past; you could easily change the future by doing that!" She glanced at me, shrugged, and walked to the doorway. Just as she was going to open the door, a light flicked on.

"Freeze!"

CHAPTER 21

— : —

CORA - THE LITTLE PRINCESS

Oliver and I froze, not moving a muscle.

"Turn around so I can see who you are, and keep your hands in the air!"

We looked at each other, both of our faces shocked, then we turned around. Grace stood in front of her bed, pointing a little wooden sword toward us. Just like the last time I saw her, her hair was red like fire and her eyes were like emeralds. If the light wasn't on, the wooden sword would've looked like a real one. When she saw Oliver's face, she tightened her grip on the sword. Then when she turned to look at me, her jaw dropped in shock.

"Gau-!"

"Wait!" I cried. Grace walked forward until she was looking right up at me.

"Cora?" She asked, her eyebrows furrowed. I glanced over at Oliver, and he gave me a 'the cat's out of the bag now' shrug. I sighed.

"Yes, I am. I'm from five hundred years in the future." Grace dropped her sword in astonishment.

"What!?! But, how do you look like you're sixteen? Do you have Delphi's Blessing? Has Malice come back? Are the protectors nice? Did you actually see Delphi when you got the blessing? Did you kick Malice's butt?" On and on she went. Oliver looked at me, trying not to laugh. Unlike me, he never knew that my sister was a very talkative, curious person. Finally, Grace took a big deep breath, her expression full of apprehension. Oliver nudged me and mouthed, "Answer her."

"Well..." I began. "Yes, I earned Delphi's Blessing, Malice does return, and no, I did not see Delphi."

"Oh." Grace's face fell, as if she expected something else. My heart dropped as I felt her disappointment wash over me, so, I leaned down and looked at her, straight in the eyes.

"But I did kick Malice's butt."

Grace's eyes widened. "Really?" I nodded. "Wow. That's awesome! Wait... But how did you even get here? Do Delphi's powers let you turn back time?"

"Well, no. We ran into a problem with a djinn, and he sent us back here."

"And we need to find a way back," Oliver added. Grace began to bite her lip.

"I think I can help you with that." She ran around to the other side of her bed and

pulled out an old, leather book with painted golden words which said: *A Wishing Guide to Counter the Magic of Djinnis and Djinns.* "I'm surprised that you don't remember this book," she said, "We've read it together over a thousand times." Grace then came back over to us and handed me the book. I flipped through the pages of the book, zigzagging left and right as I read through the text.

"It's in chapter nineteen," Grace said. Oliver helped me look through the table of contents and we found chapter nineteen. The chapter was called "How to Get Out of a Wish."

"Oh my gosh," I said. "She's right. The answer to get back is here."

"It says that a Djinn cannot leave you forever in a dream, memory, or past-like state. Instead, he is only lurking in the background watching. If you can somehow persuade him or her to free you from the wish, you are free to leave without consequences."

"But how are we supposed to find him?" Oliver asked. "It would take forever to find him in the castle. Not to mention the secret passage ways."

"I know..." I said, looking at them. "What if he's disguised? Like a guard or something?"

"Wait a second," Grace said. "There was a guard that passed by me this evening on my way back from the great hall downstairs. He didn't look the same as the other guards in the castle, but I just ran away."

"Then let's go. We need to find him as quickly as possible." We turned around and tried to leave, but Grace cried, "Wait!" We turned back and saw her fidgeting uncomfortably in place.

"What is it?" I asked.

"Do I... Do I ever get to see you again? I mean like, besides now?" I bit my lip, contemplating whether to be truthful or not. Finally, I sighed, thinking it's better to tell at least a little bit of the truth.

"Yes," I said. "You do." Grace's eyes welled with tears as she ran forward and hugged me, saying in a hoarse voice: "Thank you! Thank you! I was terrified that I would never see you again."

"I know," I said, stroking her hair. "Just... promise me that you won't say anything to anyone about this." Grace nodded and let go.

"Take it." Grace said, pointing at the music box in my hand. "The song will remind you of our family every time you listen to it." I stood there, looking long and lovingly at my sister, trying to stay strong.

"Come on," Oliver said. We left, closing the door behind us with Grace waving goodbye to me, smiling. Then, we bolted down the hallway back to the direction of where we last saw Daemon. When we got to the corridor, we began to search. First the cabinet, then the tapestries around us, then in suits of armor.

"Daemon has to be here somewhere..." So we kept searching, and searching, and searching until there was nowhere left to search. Every now and then, we had to hide as a guard or two passed. I could tell that Oliver knew I was not doing so great. My mind kept racing as I kept recounting the day of Malice's return and the terrible events that followed. I felt like I was about to have a breakdown. I finally sat down shakily on the floor and put my face in my hands. Oliver stopped what he was doing and put a hand on my shoulder to comfort me.

"Are you okay?" he asked. I shook my head. "You can talk to me. You know that." I took a huge, shaky breath, trying to not cry.

"Did the museum ever tell you how my sister died, Oliver?"

"She died the day Malice returned, right? The same day you drove Malice underground and fought him?" he asked. I nodded.

"Did they also tell you that she died getting buried alive under rubble? Holding onto her little stuffed animal bear? Her older sister, who was ten years old at the time, trying to save her life? Clawing desperately at the rocks that wouldn't move as she screamed her sister's name?" I looked at him, feeling anger, regret, and resentment all boiling inside me. "Did they ever tell you that?"

Oliver stared at me in shock and astonishment. "Oh my gosh... Cora. I... I didn't know. I'm so sorry."

"She was my Grace," I croaked, a tear rolling down my cheek "My little Amazing Grace... And I lost her because I was too late in earning my blessing. Seeing her just now, so happy to know she'd see me again..." I began to cry, burying my face into his shoulder to muffle my sound. He didn't try to stop me. Instead, he wrapped his arms around me in a tight side hug.

"It's okay," Oliver said quietly. Then he added, "It's not your fault." A loud sniff came from behind us, and we turned around to see Daemon, floating before us, wearing golden armor.

"That," Daemon said, wiping a tear from his eye, "was the saddest story in the world. The connection between you and your sister was absolutely incredible."

Oliver and I stood up as quickly as we could. "What do you want?" Oliver snarled. "Here to gloat over us being stuck here?"

"Actually, I'm not," he said, looking at me. "I'm here to help you." Our mouths dropped in shock.

"But why?" I asked, my voice cracking. "You've done nothing but try to put us all in danger."

"When you were near the island, I began to feel a presence. A presence so strong that immediately I knew that I had to have it. I have been stuck on that island for over a millenia for a crime that I did not commit. Your power was the key to my freedom, a chance to start anew. So, I wanted to take your power so I could finally be free. But..." Daemon clenched his fists. "It doesn't respond to me. It has been keeping me here. I want you to take it back, but only under one condition."

"What is that?" I asked.

"I want to be free and not stuck on this island for the rest of my life. Your power is the only thing that can free me, but I cannot do it alone. You have to do it."

I bit my lip, thinking. Then nodded. "Okay."

"What!?! Cora?" Oliver said, aghast. "You're not seriously considering this."

"We need my power in order to stop Malice, Oliver. If he's being honest, then no one deserves to be imprisoned for something they never did." I took a few steps forward and looked Daemon directly in the eye. "I promise that I will set you free... and I do keep my word." For a moment, Daemon stood there, looking a little intimidated before nodding. Then he held out his hands. I took them and immediately a brilliant golden light began to glow from Daemon's hands and slowly transfer onto mine. I sighed as I felt the familiar power of Delphi return to me. Daemon and I let go of each other's hands, taking a few steps back in the process. Power and energy radiated from me, pulsing through the air like a fierce heart beat. I slowly swished my hand through the air, creating a golden swirl of light that floated gently, as if on a breeze. Then I clenched my right fist, and the golden light disappeared.

"Alright," I said, looking at Daemon. "Now how do we get back to the actual present?"

Chapter 22

Cora - Temple on the Mountain

In a flash of orange light, Oliver and I fell right on our faces as our knees buckled from the sudden feeling of ground beneath our feet. We had arrived back on the sandy beach of Daemon's island. The sun was at its highest point in the sky as seagulls and clouds were gliding gracefully above our heads. I got up and brushed the sand from my hair and clothes.

"You better leave as soon as you can," Daemon said. "The Temple of the Sun is at the summit of the mountain that's located at the heart of the island. You'll need to head West, which will lead you straight to the temple."

"What about our friends?" Oliver asked, getting up. Daemon flicked his hand, and our friends materialized next to us, free from the chains that bound them. The guards massaged their wrists while Harper, Cyrus, and Fin checked on Racheal, who still lay unconscious on the floating platform. Then another flick of his hands, and the Staff of Light appeared at Oliver's feet. He quickly picked it up.

"Wait," I said. "Aren't you coming with us, Daemon?"

"I'm afraid I am not. Freedom is calling me from beyond this wretched island and I am eager to leave." Daemon floated closer to me and took hold of my hands. "I do wish you luck on your journey and in healing your friend." He wrung his hands. "And I'm sorry for the pain I caused you."

"Thank you, Daemon." I said, giving him a reassuring smile. "I wish you luck as well." Daemon gave me a wide smile. Then, with a wave of his hand, Daemon turned into a cloud of red smoke and disappeared into the wind.

"Alright," Oliver called out to everyone. "You heard Daemon. We better leave now and head west before it gets dark."

"Then let's go." Cryus said. And so we did, trudging through the jungle of trees, vines, and bushes. The Tribal guards used their spears and swords to slice through the brush around us as we made our way to the temple.

"Ahh!" Harper screeched.

"What is it?" Oliver asked.

"There was a giant spider that was crawling on a leaf next to me," she groaned. Fin started laughing.

"Seriously?" Fin asked, exasperated. "After all we've been through in this adventure, and you're scared of a spider?"

"For your information, Fin, that spider was about the size of my hand!" Fin snickered at Harper's retort. With a final slashing of vines, we arrived at the base of the mountain. As I looked up, I could see the mountain's summit, maybe about six thousand meters up.

"Alright," Cyrus said. "So, how are we going to get up there?"

"Cora, can you do something that can conjure stairs?" Oliver asked.

"I wish I could, but that isn't something that I can do."

"Well," Oliver said, rolling up his sleeves, "then we better start climbing."

"But how are we supposed to bring Racheal up with us?" Harper asked, gesturing to the floating platform that Racheal laid on.

"I don't know!" Oliver said, sounding defeated.

"Cora..." I jumped in surprise as a soft woman's voice whispered in my ear, echoing in my head.

"Cora, are you okay?" Fin asked. I didn't answer. Instead, I waved my hand for everyone to be quiet.

"Cora..." The voice echoed.

"There it is again," I mumbled.

"What?" Oliver asked.

"I can hear a woman saying my name," I said, looking at them.

"Listen to me. You need to do exactly what I tell you." The voice began.

"What is the woman saying?" Cyrus interrupted.

"That I need to listen to her," I said. "Now shush!"

"Find a flat surface on the side of the mountain."

"We have to find a flat surface of the mountain," I said to Oliver, Fin, Harper, and the guards. "Everyone spread out." We began to search, looking everywhere on the mountain side for anything that could relate to what the woman said.

"Princess!" a guard yelled from about twenty feet away. "I found something!" We all ran to where the guard stood to see a small, circular surface of the mountain smoothed out. It was just big enough for a hand to fit on it.

"Good," the woman said. "Now, place your hand on it. It will respond to your power." I did as I was told. I placed my hand onto the smooth surface and instantly, I felt a rush of power surge through my body as if I was struck by lightning. The rock beneath my hand began to quake and crumble, and I pulled away.

"Everybody back up!" I heard Oliver cry out. We all ran out of the way. Slowly, the mountain side began to shift and fold itself to create stairs that protruded from the mountain side, curving their way up the mountain to the top like a bunch of Zs all stacked one on top of another.

"Woah," I heard Fin say behind me.

"Go," the woman's voice said. "Remember the scroll's words. They will guide you." And just like that, the voice disappeared in a small gust of wind.

"Well," I said to the others. "I guess we better go up the mountain then."

CHAPTER 23

—— ❊ ——

OLIVER - CORA'S CRAZY IDEA

Cora led the way as we began our ascent up the mountain, trying to not trip and plummet to our deaths. Seagulls and parrots whizzed over the tree tops and around our heads like they were curious as to why humans would be up so high. I couldn't blame them. I mean, it's not everyday you see an all powerful princess with a group of people climbing up stairs that the mountain created. As we continued to get higher up, the sun slowly began to fall from the sky, making the once baby blue sky a pale peach.

Finally after some time, we reached the summit. However, it wasn't something you'd expect to see. Half of the mountain was a tall pointed top. The other half had been carved out, leaving a flat cliff that was shaped like a half circle. Cora walked over to the edge of the cliff and looked out to the island's forest and ocean view. The sun danced above the sea's waves, getting closer and closer to the ocean below.

"Wow," she said in awe.

"It's beautiful, isn't it?" I asked, walking up to stand next to her.

"Yeah. It really is."

"Hey guys!" Harper called from behind. "Check this out!" We walked back over to where everyone was standing at the center of the cliff's surface. As we got closer, I could make out markings cut into the mountain's rock, like small cuts on flesh. They seemed to make symbols that encircled the area where Harper and the others were standing.

"What is it?" Cora asked.

"More symbols like the ones from Delphi's language. They're everywhere!"

"And there's this giant hole right here," Cyrus added, pointing to where his feet were. Directly between Cyrus' feet was this hole in the shape of a diamond that must've been about the size of a computer mouse.

"Whatever was in there was definitely something big," Harper said.

"Your highness!" One of the guards said, aghast. We all turned to look at the two guards, both were standing around Racheal's unconscious body on the floating platform. Racheal's skin was now an oatmeal color, and the areas around her eyes were becoming a faint dark purple.

"She's getting worse," the other guard said. "We're running out of time."

"Okay," Cora said, her voice becoming a little panicky. "The woman said something about 'remembering the scroll's words.' So, what did the scroll say?"

No one said anything. Not even I could remember. Then Harper began to speak.

"It said: *To the one who holds the power of the sun,*

For then the battle has now truly begun.

At the last light of day,

The sun will bend your way.

Then cast the light into the dragon's eye,

And you shall see the Temple rise.

Only when mortal and immortal combine,

will then lead to a path of powers divine."

Everyone stared at her in shock.

"What?" Harper said defensively, her cheeks turning red. "I may not look like it, but I'm really good at remembering really important things."

"Uhhh…" Cora said, astonished. "Well, we've already made it to the mountain like Daemon said. So, the scroll must be on how to find this temple."

"But Daemon knew where the temple was," I said. "Couldn't he have seen it?"

"He can only sense power. It's not like he's all seeing."

"So then how are we supposed to find the temple?" I asked.

"It says: '*At the last light of day, The sun will bend your way.*' I'm guessing that that has something to do with it almost being sundown."

"Yeah, but then what?" Fin asked. "It then says: '*Cast the light into the dragon's eye.*' From what I can tell, there isn't any dragon eye anywhere."

"Maybe it means something that can represent a dragon eye," Harper said.

"Maybe like a small hole that just happens to be a certain shape? Perhaps the same shape as the bottom of the Staff of Light?" Cyrus said, looking at the floor beneath him.

"Exactly!" Harper agreed. "How did you-" Then she saw the hole between Cyrus' feet and the Staff of Light which Oliver was carrying. "Oh."

"Quick, Oliver," Cora ordered, looking at me. "Put the staff into the hole." Cyrus stepped back as I came forward and did what she ordered. It fit perfectly, but nothing happened.

"Ummm..." Harper said. "Why isn't it working?"

"Hold on," Fin said. "I have an idea." He grabbed hold of the staff and twisted it to the right. We heard the sound of a small click, and the staff lowered a little into the mountain. At that moment, the sun was perfectly in line with the staff, filling the top of the hollowed out sun that was molted to the top of the Staff of Light with its light. Suddenly, the earth shook in a violent rage as rocks tumbled to the ground from the mountain's peak above our heads. We all fell to the ground and covered our heads, trying not to get hit by the flying rubble. But as soon as it started, the rumbling stopped, which honestly surprised me at first until I heard Fin say, "Is it just me, or does it feel like the air is getting thinner?" He was right; for some reason, clouds were surrounding us from all sides, and it seemed to be getting harder to breathe. I got up and looked around. I couldn't see the island or the ocean. Instead, all I could see was a world of clouds and stars.

We were rising into the sky!

"Oh my gosh!" Harper cried, looking around. "This is insane!"

"You think that's insane?" Cyrus said. "Then look behind you!" Cora, Harper, Fin, and I turned to see the rocky mountain peak changing, creating stone columns and stairs that lead up to two stone doors that were at least one hundred feet high. A symbol of a dragon flying in front of a sun with its wings outstretched was carved into the two doors.

"It's my family's symbol," Cora muttered. "This has to be the temple."

"Come on," I said, grabbing her shoulder. "Let's get inside." Together, we walked cautiously up the stone stairs as the giant double stone doors opened to reveal a huge room the size of a ball room. The floor was made of smooth quartz, glinting in the light of torches that had mysteriously begun to spit fire into the air the moment we walked inside. In the center of the quartz floor was once again the symbol of the sun and dragon. Columns surrounded the room, reaching high above our heads to the ceiling, where more symbols were carved.

"What does the writing say?" I asked Cora.

"'Only when mortal and immortal combine, will then lead to a path of powers divine.'" Cora turned to look at me. "It's the final part of the scroll's message."

"This has to be it then," Cyrus said to us from across the temple.

"So, how does this temple work?" Harper asked Cora. Cora didn't answer at first but knelt down and placed a hand on the symbol carved into the floor. Immediately, she began to radiate golden light that spread down to the floor and all around the cracks and crevices of the temple. Cora looked up and pointed to where Harper, Fin, Cyrus, Racheal, and I were, and we all gasped in astonishment as we realized that we were glowing too. Then, Cora lifted her hand from the symbol, and everything stopped glowing.

"I think... I think I know." Cora turned to look over at the two guards and the unconscious form of Racheal. "Guards! Place Racheal in the center of the room." The two guards obeyed at once, and Cora stepped away as they took Racheal off her platform to lay her down in the center of the temple where Cora stood moments before. Then, Cora walked over to where we stood.

"Alright," she said, looking at my friends and I. "I can't do this alone. I need each of you to stand next to a column. There are five columns, and, including Racheal, that's the right amount of people.

"How are we going to help you?" Harper asked. "We don't have any special powers. Well, besides Oliver with his giant Staff of Light."

"I'm going to channel your souls into my own," Cora said, matter of factly.

"What?" We all said in unison.

"Inside of everyone is the light of a person's soul that can never be extinguished. That light is directly connected to Delphi and her power, and if I'm correct, I'm guessing that I have to fuse your mortal souls and my immortal soul together in order to harness Delphi's divine power and heal Racheal."

"But does that mean that if one of us dies, we all die?" Cyrus asked. "Like in stories?"

"No," Cora said. "As far as I know, that's never happened before."

"So, nothing bad will happen to us?" Harper clarified. Cora nodded. We all looked at each other with concerned expressions before Fin spoke.

"We have to do this," he said, looking over to where Racheal lay. "For Racheal."

"And for everyone," Harper added.

"And for each other," I said, looking at Cora. Our eyes locked, and I realized that there was more to what was about to happen than Cora let on. We all knew that this was a long shot, but Cora knew her powers better than we did, and we needed to trust her. No matter how crazy her idea sounded.

CHAPTER 24

CORA - ONE FINAL BLESSING

To be honest, when Harper, Fin, Cyrus, and Oliver agreed to do what I told them to do, I was surprised. I mean, I could have been completely wrong, and we could've all turned to ash, or exploded! But here we were; I was in the center with Racheal lying unconscious at my feet, and Harper, Fin, Cyrus, and Oliver were standing at separate columns, surrounding me and Racheal.

"Are you guys ready?" I asked.

"Whenever you are, Cora," Fin answered, giving me a reassuring smile.

"We can do this, guys," Cryus said.

"Just try not to blow us up," Harper said, her voice going up an octave.

I looked over to where Oliver was standing, looking directly at me with an anxious expression on his face. Our eyes locked once again, and I began to wonder if he had found the prophecy engraved on the locket and discovered the choice I may have to make one day. I shivered slightly at the thought, but it instantly was wiped from my mind as I spun slowly around to look at all of them. They all trusted me and had helped me through so much. The least I could do for them was to heal Racheal. I hoped this worked.

"We will be outside, your highness," one of the guards said. They left, closing the giant stone doors behind them. An eerie silence fell upon our ears as I took a deep breath.

"Let's begin," I said. Everyone nodded. With both of my hands, I began to slowly swipe through the air and create symbols with floating rays of light. I could feel power flowing through my body like a river. After some time, I knelt down and began to pray. The symbols floated around me like spirits.

Delphi, help me heal Racheal. Please.

Then something strange happened. I felt myself floating up into the air as if gravity didn't work anymore. I hovered about ten feet in the air, my feet dangling.

"Uhhh," Fin said, "is it just me, or do you guys feel strange?"

"Yeah," Harper said. "It's like stirring inside... Ah!" Harper yelped as golden light shot out her chest and into my own, creating a beam of light that connected us. The same happened to Fin, Cyrus, Oliver, and Rachael. They're bodies began to glow golden and so did the irises of their eyes. Then, the sound of a dragon's roar echoed around us, making the temple walls shake.

"What was that?" Cyrus yelled, but no one answered. Suddenly, a ghostly form of an emerald green dragon erupted from the ground;

its transparent green scales magically shimmered in the golden light. Instead of attacking us, it began to circle me, protecting me from any harm that might come to me. The dragon stared at me with a content look on its face. I could feel myself becoming drowsy, as if I was being hypnotized, and I blacked out.

When I woke up, I was lying face up in a grassy meadow. I could hear the sound of grasshoppers and birds chirping. The sky was a pale blue, fluffy white clouds glided silently above my head, and the sun was perched high above me in the sky. I looked around, trying to figure out how I had gotten from the temple to here when I realized that I wasn't wearing my torn up outfit the Tribe had given me. Instead, I wore a white silk dress that was knee length in the front and draped down to the ground in the back. I still wore the golden belt, but also brown leather boots, chest armor, leg armor, and a helmet that painfully pushed my crown against my forehead. Tied around my waist was a leather scabbard with a long, golden sword that glinted in the fierce sunlight.

"Where am I?" I muttered to myself. A sudden movement out of the corner of my eye made me whip around. There, the same dragon that had encased me in the temple stood, staring me down with it's green and gold eyes.

"You brought me here, didn't you?" I asked. The dragon didn't do anything. Instead, the dragon turned and ran through the meadow.

"Hey!" I yelled, running after the dragon. "Come back!" The dragon's feet thudded a rhythmic pattern on the ground as we raced across the field. The farther we ran, the more tired I became. The armor was weighing me down as if I was carrying the world on my shoulders. *How on earth did the guards of the Crystal Falls Palace survive in this armor?* Then in the back of my mind, I heard the same woman's voice as before speak to me.

"In order to find one's true self, one must let go of the heavy burden of the past." This gave me an idea. As I ran, I unstrapped the armor from my body, and it clattered onto the grassy earth, clanging against itself. The loss of the armor made me feel as light as a feather, allowing me to speed up to a sprint. As I reached out to try and grab the dragon's back, a forest appeared out of nowhere. I skidded to a halt.

"What the..." I watched as the dragon weaved its way through the trees and brush. I tried to make my way through the woods, but it was as if the branches of the trees were trying to grab my waist, pulling me back. I reached for my golden sword and sliced through the branches. That seemed to agitate the forest, making the trees sway violently in an invisible breeze.

"Let go of the violent urge to fight," I heard the woman's voice say. "Sometimes, it is better to let the world help you and guide you in the right direction."

I took a deep breath and reluctantly dropped my sword and unlatched my scabbard from my waist. I let myself relax, and immediately the branches lifted me into the air and carried me through the forest, the trees taking turns to carry me through the woods. Then, about twenty feet ahead of me, I could see, once again, the dragon running in front of me. The trees lowered me to the ground and pushed me forward allowing me to start running again. I leapt over a log and reached the base of a mountain. The dragon had already begun its ascent, clawing its way up the mountain's jagged rock. I followed, climbing higher and higher. At one point, I reached out to grab a rock that jutted out, but it broke and cut my palm open. My hand began to sting painfully as blood oozed from it. I ignored it and kept climbing until finally I pulled myself up onto the top of the mountain, gasping for air. As I looked around, I saw the endless sea surrounding the mountain. The forest and grassy meadow had somehow disappeared. To my right, the emerald dragon had stopped, looking out where the sky and sea met. I took two steps forward, and the dragon turned it's head to look at me.

"Why did you bring me here?" I asked. The dragon grunted, sending golden smoke out of it's nostrils. I took two more steps forward. "Are you the divine power the scroll mentioned?" A few more steps. "If that's the case... why did you choose me?" Now, I was only ten feet away from the dragon. My breath was coming in and out sharply as my heart pounded against my chest. I took one more step forward, and instantly I wished that I hadn't. The dragon whipped around and dove off of the mountain side. "No!" I yelled. I ran forward but stopped as the half of the mountain side gave way, leaving a cliff. Dragon wings materialized on the dragon's back, and it soared off into the sunset, disappearing.

"Get back here!" I hollered. Nothing happened. I kicked a rock, and it skittered off the ledge of the cliff.

What am I supposed to do? I sat down at the edge of the cliff and looked out to watch the sun sink quickly through the sky and touch the sea.

"Do not let the sun go down on your anger," the woman's voice whispered in the wind. "Sometimes, the hardest choice you have to make is the one that will help you succeed in your journey."

And finally I understood. The armor, the sword, the forest, everything. This wasn't to help Racheal, at least, not exactly. It had all been a test to see if I was worthy. Worthy enough to wield a power that I had already earned but only recently had begun to understand. I knew exactly what to do.

I got up, turned around, walked back over to one side of the mountain cliff, and braced myself for what I knew I had to do. I knelt down into a sprinting position and propelled myself forward, running as fast as my legs could carry me before I pushed off the ledge, plummeting towards the sea.

The emerald dragon suddenly materialized below me and skyrocketed upward, wrapping its wings around me. Green and golden light filled my vision as the dragon roared. A new feeling of power that I never felt before began to stir inside me, and I realized whose voice I had been hearing.

"I have waited eons for this day to come," Delphi's voice said in my ear. "I could never be more proud of a descendant. You have earned my final blessing."

CHAPTER 25

—— ◆ ——

OLIVER - HARPER'S BROTHER.

Even though nothing looked different, I knew that something was happening inside Cora's mind. Cora's body hovered about ten feet from the ground. Her hair swirled as if she was caught in a strong wind storm. It was also as if time had slowed down around her. As I watched, she mouthed a word: "Delphi," soundlessly pronouncing it within the silence as the spirit of the dragon weaved its way around her.

"When do you think this is going to end?" Cyrus called over to me, gesturing to the rays of light that were shooting out of our chests.

"Whenever Cora can heal Racheal I guess."

"Guys look!" Harper yelled. "Something's happening!" I looked up and gasped as the dragon began to circle around all of us. It was so close that I could've reached out to touch it, but I didn't. It gave a low grumble, leapt up, and flew right into Cora, going inside of her. Then there was a flash of light that blinded all of us, and a loud roar nearly blasted my ear drums. When the light faded, Cora floated down as if in slow motion. I ran forward, holding out my arms, and caught Cora, setting her down gently next to Racheal.

"Oh my gosh!" Harper shrieked.

"Cora," I said, shaking her. "Cora, are you okay?" She didn't answer at first. Then with a small groan, her eyes fluttered open, and she sat up, clutching her head.

"How are you feeling?" I asked her.

"Strange," she said. "Like I hit my head against a rock but also like I could throw Malice a hundred miles."

"Well at least you're okay," I said, smiling.

"But what about Racheal?" Harper asked. Cora looked over to her left to see Racheal still lying there unconscious.

"I think I can finally heal her," Cora said. She reached out her arm and placed her hand next to the dagger lodged in Racheal's leg, closing her eyes. Almost at once, the dagger turned to ash, falling away onto the floor as the blood on Racheal's clothes disappeared and the wound healed itself, leaving unblemished skin. Racheal's face regained its normal color, and she sighed in her sleep. "There," Cora said, opening her eyes. "She'll be fine now. Just give her a minute." Racheal then sat up slowly, blinking and rubbing her eyes as she looked around, a confused expression on her face.

"What happened?" she asked. "Where on earth are we?"

"A lot has happened since you were stabbed," I replied, smiling. Racheal looked at me with wide eyes the moment I said the word "stabbed." "But we'll explain all of it later. Right now, we have to find a way to get off this mountain and back home."

"I can do that," Harper and Cora said in unison. Both looked at each other before smiling.

"I can get the temple back down," Cora said.

"And I know someone who can get us back home," Harper said. "You do one, and I'll do the other."

"Deal," Cora agreed. So, the two split off. Cora got up and walked over to the right side of the wall while Harper walked over to the left wall, pulled out her phone, and began to speak to someone. I watched as Cora placed her right hand on the wall, and once again the temple quaked as we were lowered back to the island's surface. With one final earthquake, I got up and together, we all walked out of the temple, supporting Racheal, who was still a little weak in the knees. When we got outside, we saw the two guards talking to one another, looking terrified. When they saw us, they bowed before getting up.

"Your highness," one of the guards said. "You are alright! And your friend is safe! Thank Delphi!"

"But we need to leave," the other guard interrupted. "Something is happening in Crystal Falls."

"What?" Cora said. "What are you talking about?"

"The chief sent us a message." He pointed to a charm he wore around his neck. "This charm is how the chief can communicate to us from far away. He said that there was a major disturbance in Malice's energy. He's becoming increasingly agitated."

"Send a message back saying that we'll be back as soon as possible," Cora commanded. "Malice must know that we have everything that we need."

"But how will we get back?" Fin asked.

"I took care of that," Harper said, stepping forward. "My brother owns a pretty big boat. I told him our location, and he said that he'll be here soon."

"Is that who you were calling?" I asked Harper. She nodded.

"What's he like?" Cora asked.

"He's sweet, he's always there, and he makes you laugh so hard that you-"

"I hate to break up this small chat," Fin interjected, "but we need to find our way back to the beach. Let's go before it gets so dark that we can't see anything." Even though it was night, it wasn't dark at all. The light from the full moon above our heads seemed to go straight through the leaves and branches of the trees and shine down upon us, lighting the way. Stars glittered above our heads as we walked back through the chopped down brush that the guards had cut down earlier that day. After a while, we arrived back on the soft sandy beach that outlined the island. Our fire must have been washed out by the tide because all that was left of it was a few twigs and burnt palm leaves.

"So," Cyrus said, looking around. "Do we just sit here and wait or…"

"There he is!" Harper cried pointing to the left. Out on the horizon was a small bright dot of light that was slowly getting bigger as it neared. As it got closer, I could see the glittering black lightning bolt painted against a red boat's side in the moonlight. It was at least thirty feet long with a set of Mercury six hundred horsepower V12 engines. Milk white leather seats ringed the inside of the boat's interior where a tall twenty-five year old man stood, waving at us and smiling widely. The boat stopped out in the water, its engine still humming as the man motioned for us to get on. We all waded out in the water and climbed in. The man handed us red and white towels, and we started to dry off. The man, or Harper's brother as I know him now, wore a red leather jacket and beanie with a white shirt, black jeans and red tennis shoes. He had shaggy blonde hair and steel gray eyes.

"I'm glad I got your call, sis," Harper's brother said, hugging her. "But how on earth did you get here without a boat or a plane?"

"We did have a boat, but it's a long story," Harper said dismissively.

"Well, you better start telling!" Harper's brother demanded, pointing at all of us. "All of your parents have been worried sick about you. The entire town has!"

"Wait," Cora said, looking at the man. "So, you're Harper's brother?"

"The one and only!" he said, looking at Cora. "And you're the girl that was on the news. The one found at the museum, right?"

"Yes."

"Well, my name is Tyler Mathew Hayes, but you can just call me Tyler."

CHAPTER 26

CORA - CAMP CRYSTAL FALLS

No one talked on the boat ride, not even Tyler or Harper seemed to want to speak to each other. It was strange. Shouldn't siblings always talk to each other? Harper sounded so fond of him. Tyler parked the boat next to a wooden platform that was attached to the land in front of us. He tied a rope to a wooden post and helped us off, one by one.

"We must leave," the two guards said. "It has been an honor to be in your presence, your highness." They bowed to me before turning and disappearing into a patch of trees.

"Whoever those guys are, I like them." Tyler said. "They respect you, Princess..."

"Cora," I said to Tyler. "Cora Williams."

"Wait, like the one that was supposed to be alive over five hundred years ago?" We all nodded, and Tyler's mouth dropped. "But aren't you supposed to be dead?"

"Like I said, Tyler, there is a lot to explain." Harper said, hugging him tightly. "But right now we need someplace safe. Can you take us to camp?"

"I mean, sure, but I need to call all of your parents to let them know I found you."

"Don't!" I said. At that same moment, a painful burst of power shot through my body, making me double over in pain as an image of Malice flashed in my mind.

"Cora, are you alright?" Oliver asked.

"The chief was right," I said. "Malice knows what I've done, and he's angry... or planning something. I'm not sure." Tyler stood there for a moment, biting his lip and scanning me up and down like he still didn't believe I was real.

"Fine," he said. "I won't tell anyone yet. I trust that you and your friends know what you're doing. Now let's get to the car and you can tell me everything on the way." So, he led us down a path to where he had parked his car, and he got inside. The car had a black exterior and red leather seats that were really comfortable. "Buckle up!" Tyler said from the driver's seat. He turned on the car, and we sped off down the road.

The stars danced high above our heads as we flew down what Oliver said was a highway. Harper, Oliver, Cyrus, Fin, Racheal, and I explained everything about what had happened within the past few days before Tyler interrupted.

"A few days!?!" He said, shocked. "Do you guys have any idea how long it has actually been?"

"Yeah!" Oliver said. "It's only been like five days."

"No..." Tyler argued. "It's been over two weeks since you guys went missing."

"What?" Racheal said, astonished. "How is that possible?"

"Perhaps time is different on Daemon's island," I said. Tyler got off the highway and turned right onto a dirt road lined with trees on both sides. On and on it went, looking as if it could go on forever before the tree line disappeared to be replaced by a beautiful array of wooden cabins that were all scattered around the area. Some were made of walnut, others were made of dark hickory. Different assortments of cars were parked next to these cabins. Each cabin had a dark green painted door and large windows. Even though the windows of both the cabin and car were shut, in the back of my mind I could hear what was going on inside as if part of my soul was inside the cabins. A baby crying as a mother sang them to sleep, a child laughing as their father chased them around, both shooting fake multicolored darts at each other. A husband and wife swaying to the soft sounds of music from a radio.

"We're here," Tyler said, parking the car. I turned to look at what he was talking about and saw a giant three story cabin made of eastern white pine, one of my father's favorite types of wood, with double wooden doors and giant windows scattered along the walls of the cabin mansion.

"Is this where you live?" I asked Tyler.

"Yep," he said. "This place is Camp Crystal Falls. I own the entire campground."

"Wow…" I said, astonished.

"Please, come inside," he said, opening the two doors to let us in. After a tour of the place and going through so many rooms that I lost count, Tyler led us back to the living room where there was a giant white couch with a bear pattern blanket. "Okay," Tyler said, clapping his hands together. "You guys are gonna have to share the couch and the two guest rooms upstairs."

"Thank you, but we aren't staying," I said.

"I thought we were," Harper countered.

"We can't! We have to find Malice before he starts looking for us."

"Cora," Cyrus said, flopping onto the couch. "Malice hasn't done anything catastrophic yet. Let's just take a break. We've all been through a lot, and we aren't going to be able to fight if we're all tired." Anger flared up inside of me, but I took a deep breath.

"You're right, Cyrus," I said. "Let's just sit down. It's not like Malice can destroy an entire town in one swoop. Oh wait, he can!"

"Okay, stop it, you two," Fin said, standing up. "Cora, we all understand how important it is to stop Malice, but please, try to understand that we don't have as much 'stamina' as you. Let's just rest tonight, and then we'll begin our search. Hopefully we're right and Malice won't start looking right away." I clenched my fists, feeling Delphi's power slowly building up inside of me. Then I felt a soft hand grab mine, and I turned to see Oliver looking at me.

"Come on. Let's go take a walk." Then he turned to look at the others. "You guys rest. We'll join you in a few minutes." They all nodded. Oliver led me out of the cabin and out into the soft green grass. A light breeze swirled around us as Oilver and I walked around for roughly ten minutes before we arrived at a cliff that dropped down into the sea. The sound of crashing waves filled my ears as we sat down on a wooden bench that could've fit three people.

"Why did you bring me out here?" I asked Oliver, still a little angry.

"Well, it seemed to me that you needed a little time away from everyone. Sometimes, we just need space from others."

"I appreciate it, Oliver, but I won't stop until Malice is destroyed. I have to keep going."

Silence.

"Ummm, Cora?"

"What?" I answered. Oliver shifted uncomfortably on the bench.

"I know it's not my place to ask, but what happened in the temple? I mean, I saw the dragon and the light, but something else happened to you. Can you tell me?"

At first, I didn't know how to answer. I kinda felt like I wanted to lie and say that nothing happened, but I couldn't.

"There's too much to explain..."

"Please explain," he said, looking into my eyes. "I'll listen to you."

"Let's... Let's just say that I understand the power of Delphi now," I said, creating a golden wisp of light that floated gently in the air that formed my family's royal symbol. His eyes widened like he understood what I meant. Suddenly, the sky began to turn blood red as if a drop of red paint had dripped onto a painter's masterpiece, seeping slowly and deliberately through the bends and folds of the wet paint. The wind howled and whipped around us, smacking my hair against my face.

"What is happening?" Oliver yelled. I tensed as I felt a dark, cold presence fill the air.

"We need to get back!" I yelled. "Run!" I clutched desperately to Oliver's hand as we dashed through the forest, pulling him along. Branches of trees tugged and tore at my clothes as if urging me to let go of Oliver's hand and stay there, but I couldn't. A loud roar filled the air as we continued running. Birds took flight from the safety of the trees, flying over our heads.

"This is exactly like my dream!" Oliver yelled over the chaos.

"What!?!"

"Before I met you, I had a dream almost exactly like this! Except I tripped and broke my foot-"

"Well right now is not the time! We need to get back!" An evil, hissing laughter rose in the air and echoed around us, making goosebumps rise all over my skin. When we arrived back at the campground, I saw Tyler, Harper, Racheal, Cyrus, and Fin bolting out of the cabin mansion toward us.

CHAPTER 27

OLIVER - HOW TO SAVE A TOWN

"What the heck is going on?" Cyrus yelled.

"Malice, he's looking for us!" I said.

"And he'll destroy everything in the process!" Cora added. "We need to get everyone from Crystal Falls here!"

"Why?" Tyler asked.

"Because here I can create a barrier that can stop Malice from getting into the campground. It will take a lot of my energy, but it will work."

"But by the time we would get to Crystal Falls, Malice could have destroyed half the town!" Harper argued. "How on earth are we going to tell everyone that fast?"

"I got it!" Racheal said. "Everyone pull out your phone. Start posting! Quickly!" Everyone, except for Cora, pulled out their phones and began to post on every social media platform that we knew.

"That should do it," I said, looking at them all. "Now all we have to do is wait."

"There's not enough time," Cora said. "Oliver, grab my hand!" I looked at her confused. "Trust me!" I put my hand into hers. "What does the town look like?" she asked. I quickly described what Crystal Falls looked like before Cora nodded. "Got it!" In a flash of golden light we materialized in the center of Crystal Falls. Restaurants, bars, and an assortment of shops lined both sides of the town. Because it was dark, not many people were on the street, just the occasional drunk adult or teenager skateboarding down the sidewalk.

"How on earth did you get us here?" I asked, looking around.

"I just imagined what you described Crystal Falls as," Cora said. "Besides, we need to let people know what's going on."

"Umm..." I said, looking behind us down the street. "I don't think that we need to worry about that." I pointed to where we could see almost every single elder, child, parent, and teen running for their life as they fled down the street away from a giant mass of magenta and black smoke. The smoke swirled to make a giant dome, slowly getting bigger and bigger as it consumed everything in its path.

"Everyone!" Cora yelled to the crowd. "Get to Camp Crystal Falls now!" Cora and I joined the crowd of people as we began the three mile run down the street and towards the camp, running as fast as our legs could carry us. I turned to look back through the swarm of people, trying to see through them and find my parents.

191

"No!" someone screamed. Loud screams filled the air as five, no, six people were sucked into the smoke, crying out for help as they disappeared.

"Keep moving!" Cora cried. "Faster!" Parents scooped up their children into their arms as we picked up our speed and sprinted into the camp, the smokey dome getting closer and closer to the front of the crowd.

"Cora!" I yelled. "Start creating the shield!" Cora stopped behind the crowd and clapped her hand together, sending an arc of light into the sky. She began to emanate golden light that lit up the entire campsite. Above all of our heads, a shield of light began to expand around us, touching the ground.

"Wait!" a woman cried. "My son!" I turned around and saw one little boy, about the age of ten, running towards us as fast as his little legs could take him. However, I knew that by the time he could get here, the cloud would've already consumed us.

"He's not gonna make it!" Cyrus yelled, running to us as Tyler and the rest of our friends followed behind. "He can't run fast enough!" No one said anything. Then, Tyler turned to look at Harper and hugged her.

"Tyler," Harper said, "what are you..?" She stopped short as Tyler let go of her and ran as fast as he could towards the boy, breaking through an opening of the shield.

"Tyler, no!" but Tyler ignored Racheal's cry. He picked up the boy in his arms and sprinted back to us.

"Oliver!" Cora yelled from behind me. I turned, her face was turning pale and she looked completely exhausted. "I have to complete the shield! I can't leave an opening or Malice will get inside!"

"Just hold on a little longer!" I called back, but I knew she was right. At that moment, Tyler tripped on a root, and there was a sound like a gunshot. He and the boy went down. When Tyler tried to get back up, he yelled in pain and fell to the ground. His foot must have broken, just like mine had in my dream.

"Go!" He yelled to the little boy. The boy sprinted as fast as he could and made it inside of the barrier, wrapping his arms around his mother, sobbing.

"Tyler!" Harper yelled. She ran forward, but Cryus and I grabbed her and held her back. Tyler looked at Harper and smiled.

"I love you, Harper." Tyler said, smiling. "You were the best little sister I could've asked for." Then the smoke engulfed him, and we watched, horrified, as Tyler turned to ash and became one with Malice's dome.

"Noo!" Harper screamed and collapsed onto the ground, crying and wailing.

"Oliver... I can't..." Cora passed out from exhaustion and thudded to the ground.

"Cora!" I ran over. She didn't respond. I checked her pulse, which beat steadily against my fingertips. Someone screamed as a shadowy figure of a serpent dragon loomed high above our heads. There was a loud roar and something long, like a serpent's tail, collided with Cora's shield that had finally encased the campground, making a loud thud. "It's Malice!" I yelled to the others. "He's trying to get in!" Another thud and golden glitter floated down and landed on our hair. Then there was another loud roar and the shadowy figure and smoke disappeared, leaving nothing but the night sky.

"Tyler," Cora mumbled, her eyes fluttering open, "what happened?"

"He's dead, Cora," I said. "He... got caught in Malice's smoke and he turned to ash."

"What?" Cora got up and looked around. "Is Harper okay?"

"She's over there with the others." I pointed to our left. Cora rushed over and knelt down next to Harper, who was hugging Racheal.

"Harper, I'm so sorry." Harper took a huge, shaky breath and looked out to where Tyler had disappeared.

"It's okay," she said, though she didn't sound like she believed it herself. "He died a hero..." We helped her up and hugged her in the eerie silence. Then Harper muttered in our ears, "but Malice is going to pay."

CHAPTER 28

⸺ ⁂ ⸺

CORA - SUNRISE

The morning sun rose high over the campground and dew drops on the grass beneath my feet glittered like jewels. In other words, it was a perfect morning.

Except there was one problem:

A war was about to start.

It had been two days since Malice's attack, and I was standing near the cliff that dropped fifty feet into a crashing sea. The smell of salt filled my nostrils, and the warm feeling of the sun on my skin made me realize that I never really appreciated the sea until now. In fact, I had never really taken in the full beauty of the world around me. Trees swayed to the music of the wind as it whistled through the leaves and birds sang along to the tune. I looked down at the locket I was fidgeting in my hands. It was a golden heart, and in the center it read:

"To the best big sister ever.

Be yourself!

-Grace"

Instantly, I felt as if I went back in time again. I was back in the castle and running down a long corridor. I was running so fast that instead of feeling my feet hit the ground, I felt like I was flying. A loud, piercing roar rang through the castle. The roof shook violently and a wall to my left crumbled into dust. I didn't stop but kept running as screams pierced the air like bullets.

"Cora! Help!"

"Grace, I'm coming! Just hang on!"

I turned the corner and bolted down another passageway. I heard guards yell and maids scream as they were buried alive in rubble. Soldiers lay wounded on the ground, covered in a magenta and black goo that slowly oozed its way around their bodies like a boa constrictor wrapping around its prey. The roof shook again and more yells and shouts erupted around me.

Finally, I stood in front of a doorway, my eyes frantically searching for any signs of life. There, sitting in the corner of the room and clutching a teddy bear was my little sister, Grace. Her red hair was disheveled, and she had a long gash on her cheek. Tears were streaming down her face like two waterfalls, and her emerald dress was torn and covered in dust.

"You're going to be fine!" I said over another loud roar. I ran in and held out my hand. "Come on!" Grace took hold of my hand and together, we ran toward the doorway. Another roar, much louder than before, made the castle shake. A loud creaking came from above. Within that second, time seemed to slow down. As the roof came crashing down from above, Grace tripped, and her hand slipped from mine.

"Cora!" I stopped in the hallway and turned, watching as Grace's terrified face was buried beneath dust and rubble. I stood there for a moment, terrified.

"No!" I knelt down and started digging through the rubble. Hot tears streaming down my face. "Grace! Where are you!?! Say something! Grace!" There was another loud roar, and anger and pain flared up inside me. Suddenly, golden light swirled around my ten-year-old body, filling me with power that pulsed through my veins.

"Cora? Cora? Cora." Another loud roar, and I felt a hand grasp my shoulder. My eyes snapped open, and I turned to see Oliver looking at me. His expression was worried, and I didn't understand why until I looked at my hands, which were glowing gold.

"Oh. Hi, Oliver." I said, shaking my hands frantically to make the glowing fade away.

"Are you ok?"

"Yeah. Just. . . Thinking. . ." He looked at me, trying to read my thoughts.

"You're thinking about your Grace, aren't you?" I looked away toward the crashing sea. I nodded.

"It's haunted me ever since this whole thing started. When I finally earned Delphi's blessing, when I fought Malice for those five hundred years, when I got my memory back, when we protected the town and saved Rachael's life... When Tyler died... Even now, I can feel all of them watching me. But..."

"What?"

"I'm worried, Oliver. What if I fail? What if it comes down to this, and I don't succeed? They all would have died in vain. What then?"

"Then I guess we'll keep fighting," Oliver said, hugging me. "Just because you lost the first time doesn't mean you will again."

"Thank you, Oliver."

"Yeah, no problem." We stood there, silent for one moment, our eyes locked together. He leaned forward, and I pushed him away.

"What are you doing?" I asked sharply. He leaned away quickly and blushed.

"Um... Nevermind."

Silence once more.

"You know," I said, trying to change the subject while looking up at a seagull that had begun to fly above us. "My father once told me that seagulls were guides for sailors. They help them find their way back home. Maybe, maybe it's a good omen that everything is going to be okay and that our home will be safe."

"Yeah," Oliver agreed. The seagull screeched loudly as it glided away, landing on a rock below.

"Guys." Oliver and I turned to see Harper, Fin, Cyrus, Rachael and the remaining people of the town standing behind us, all of them looking worried about what lies ahead.

"Everyone wants to help in the assault on Malice," Fin said, rolling up his sleeves. "We're just waiting for your signal, Cora."

"We've already gone through the plan," Rachael continued. "We know what's at stake. We know that... we might not come back." We stood there in uncomfortable silence as if a blanket had fallen over us. Finally, Oliver took a deep breath.

"Alright. Let's go." No one spoke as we marched toward the edge of the campsite. Our footsteps thudded against the ground like thunder. Looking behind me, I could see Fin and Cyrus looking at each other with worried expressions. Rachael and Harper were both trying not to look at each other. I turned back to face forward with Oliver. His face was as pale as a sheet of paper.

I couldn't do this to them.

"Wait!" Everyone stopped and looked at me as I turned around and looked at them all. "You guys don't have to do this. I know that you want to help, but this is dangerous. You could die."

"So?" Cyrus asked, shrugging.

"So this isn't a fictional story or one of those video games Fin has talked about!" I said, looking directly at him. "This is the real world. It's not like you get killed and then come back to life."

"We know that, Cora," Harper said calmly. She put a hand on Cyrus' shoulder and looked at me. "We understand the possible consequences of our actions, but we still want to help. Malice is using our town as a fortress, remember? Our friends and families are stuck in that place, and we've lost people we really care about." She gulped down a wave of tears at the thought of Tyler. "We will do whatever it takes to save whoever is still alive."

"Here! Here!" Fin shouted, raising his fist high into the air. The people of Crystal Falls all whooped and hollered in agreement, raising their fists into the air as well. My face became hot, and my eyes started to water. I wiped the tears away.

"Alright then," I said, my voice getting a little louder. "Who's ready to kick Malice's butt?" Roars of approval rose from everyone, echoing in the silent morning sky. We continued to march, finally stopping at the edge of the barrier that kept us safe from the town about three miles away.

"Cora, do your thing," Fin whispered. I walked closer to the barrier, taking deep breaths. I could hear something like a faint humming from the barrier I had created. I raised my hand to the golden wall and touched the golden substance. At once, it disintegrated into a golden ash and blew away in the breeze. Silence. Then suddenly, far off in the distance, faint outlines of undead warriors and creatures of all sorts began to appear at the edge of Crystal Falls. Some were tall, some short, others were carrying weapons or standing next to cannons.

"Is everyone ready?" I called. All of them nodded. I raised both of my hands into the sky and golden weapons of all sorts appeared in all of our hands and armor formed around everyone's chests and legs. Everyone looked at one another in awe. "Charge!" I screamed. A roar erupted from both armies as we charged at each other. Swords clashed as arrows and spears flew like birds through the air. Within an instant, I realized that we were outnumbered. A tall, scaly creature with four arms crashed into me. I struggled as it pinned me by the throat. My lungs screamed for air, and blood roared in my ears. Out of the corner of my eye, I saw Oliver stab the creature with the staff...

But nothing happened.

The creature kept its grip on my neck, slowly crushing my windpipe. I finally was able to slash my hand through the air, and in a flash of light, the creature disintegrated into dust.

"You ok?" Oliver asked, yelling over the battle around us. He reached out, grasped my arm, and pulled me up.

"Yeah, I'm fine," I said, brushing off the creature's dust from my clothes. I looked around at the chaos before me and saw our army was in trouble. Some people lay on the ground dead, arrows and spears pierced through their golden armor and lodged themselves in their chest, making the victims look like porcupines. Other people were carrying other soldiers away from the fight back to the camp to be treated; many were fighting for their lives.

"We have to help them." I started to move toward a crowd of people that were surrounded by creatures with axes and swords. The earth quaked as another war cry rose around us. It didn't come from either army though.

It came from below.

Suddenly, warriors dressed in golden armor and dragon tiki masks erupted from the ground followed by Chief Ansel, Chayton, and Prince Dakota, all carrying different weapons. Prince Dakota saw me and smiled.

"We're here to help!" he yelled over the battle. He threw his spear, and it hit an undead soldier right in the chest.

"Warriors!" Chayton yelled. "In the name of Delphi, attack!" Oliver grabbed my arm again and pulled me away as an undead warrior slashed at me. He stabbed the undead warrior, and it burst into ash.

"We need to keep moving," Oliver said. "The Tribe of the Rising Sun is here to help. They'll be fine." Oliver yelled something incomprehensible over the cries and yells of the battle, and within an instant, Cyrus, Rachael, Fin, and Harper appeared next to me. We raced through the three armies, dodging arrows and slashing through the enemy line. Every now and then, I saw one of our own fall as a monster lunged at them. I slashed my hand through the air, and the creatures turned to dust.

We finally made it through the enemy line. Standing before us was a black matter shield that encased Crystal Falls like a lid over a pan. We walked closer to the shield until we were less than three feet away. Oliver looked at me as if telling me to come forward. I nodded and walked until I was almost pressed against it. I felt power flowing through my veins as I glowed gold once more. I raised my hand and touched the shield. The shield opened wide enough for us to walk through one at a time. With a sudden lurch in my gut, I realized that Malice's barrier was fighting back. I raised my other hand, trying to keep the barrier open.

"Go! I can't hold it much longer!" They rushed in, and I lowered my hands, diving into the open gap just as it was about to close. Everything went dark and quiet.

"We're inside, but I can't see anything." Harper started to move to the left and I heard a loud, "Ouch!" as Harper whacked Rachael in the face.

"Hang on a second..." I conjured a glowing golden orb in my hand and threw it into the air. Within seconds, the town was illuminated in the orb's glowing light.

"Thanks," Oliver said. "Now let's go."

❧❧❧❧❧ ❦❦❦❦❦

As we ran, we saw the remains of buildings and houses that had once been whole. Rubble covered the streets, making us climb over it all. We saw bodies that covered the ground. Some were only limbs that stuck out from beneath the rubble, magenta black goo covering what was left of them.

"Well, this is nice," Fin said sarcastically. "I like what Malice's done to the place." Everyone groaned. We pressed on, ignoring the possibility nagging at us that those people were still alive and needed help. If this works, we could focus on those people and hopefully save them.

We finally got close to the gates of the castle. In front of the gate was a large broken sign that read, "The Museum of Crystal Falls: Home of the Royal Family."

"Where are Malice's guards?" Harper whispered.

"Probably fighting against our side," I answered. Fin knelt down and put his hands together, creating a step. One by one, we each placed our foot in his hand and he lifted us over the gate. When I was the last one with Fin, I grabbed his hand and together in a flash of light, we appeared next to the others on the other side of the gate.

"Well that's one thing that went right so far," Harper said, looking around. The minute she said it, two scaly monsters appeared in front of us. They were covered in magenta black goo and held two long, double edged katanas. The monsters growled at us as a weird acid color slime oozed out of their mouths.

"Eww!" Harper said, disgusted.

"Well, this is it," Cyrus muttered, raising his sword to fight. "Nice knowing you guys."

"Don't say that! We got this," Oliver said, raising his staff.

"Oliver's right. We have to have faith." I raised my hand and a golden sword that glowed a faint white appeared in my hand. The creatures began circling us, trying to find our weak points.

"Harper and Rachael, you take these guys," I said. "The rest of you break off and follow me!"

"On it!" Racheal said, her voice a little higher than normal. The monsters rushed us. Rachael and Harper slashed and whirled with their spears. Harper stabbed one of the creatures, and with a high screech, it disintegrated into golden powder. When Fin, Cyrus, Oliver, and I got through the fight, we bolted up the broken stairs and pushed the entrance door open to the castle museum. Standing there was a creature that made goosebumps rise on my arms. It was as tall as the castle itself and had six arms. Its body looked like it was made of different kinds of flesh melted and sewn together, and its eyes were a fiery orange. The creature carried two, long, horrible obsidian scythes that had the unmistakable red stains of blood. I took a few steps back in shock. Fin saw me and patted me on the back.

"Cyrus and I will take care of him, Cora. You and Oliver go."

"Come on, Cora!" Oliver said, grabbing me. The creature turned and growled. It raised one scythe, but Fin shot a volley of arrows at it. The monster roared in agony as the arrows pierced its chest, causing it to stumble backward.

"Cyrus, take him from behind!" Fin ordered. Oliver and I ran past before the monster could focus on us. We immediately turned right and entered the vast, open area of the outside garden. A memory flashed through my mind as I pictured my sister and I crying as we shook the dead body of our mother.

"We made it," Oliver puffed, clutching his chest and snapping me back to reality. "But where's Malice?" A dark chasm stood in the center of the garden. I walked until my feet were at the ledge.

"I don't remember this being here. When did this happen?"

"Maybe when the Emergency Responders found us?" Oliver said, walking up next to me. "Cyrus, Racheal, Fin, and Harper said it was all over the news. Our entire school watched as we got pulled out of the chasm created by Malice's earthquake and were taken to the hospital."

"Well, that does make sense; the garden was right above the dungeons where it was said that Malice was hidden. I continued to stand there, transfixed, like a predator assessing its prey. I felt the ground disappear as a flash of light illuminated the world around me. I gasped in horror. I realized that I was standing at the bottom of the chasm, looking up at a vast, open sky. "Oliver!?!" I hollered. "Get me out of here!" My voice echoed around the chasm. No response. *Where was he?* I looked around, my eyes adjusting to the darkness. When I looked to my left, I saw two figures lying on the ground, not moving.

"Oh, my gosh."

I ran over to the figure and knelt down. That's when I realized that it was me. It must have been when Malice had escaped. I could see the bruises and scratches on my arms and face as my eyes roamed my past self's body. Next to me was Oliver, wearing a crumpled pair of jeans, a green T-shirt that said "CJ's Bowling Alley", and a pair of black socks with red tennis shoes. He was bleeding from his forehead, and there were gashes all over his body. His right hand was stretched out like he was reaching for mine. I know that I have already been in the past and have seen myself... but still... this was super weird.

A loud noise came from above, and I looked up. A flying vehicle with a spinning top was above my head. Rope sprouted from its sides, and two men slid down it. I backed away as they came close to my unconscious self. They both wore navy blue outfits with lime green stripes. On their backs, three letters were stitched across their shirts spelling, "EMT." One pulled out a walkie talkie and put it close to his mouth.

"Emergency! We have two 123s! One female and one male. Both are possible minors. Maybe seventeen or eighteen. They need medical attention immediately! Lower the gurneys!" Two long, thin beds were lowered, and very carefully, the two men carried Oliver's and my unconscious bodies and placed us onto the beds. Then in a flash of light, I appeared back at the edge of the chasm. Oliver had grabbed my waist, trying to keep me from falling. He slowly tugged me a few steps backward.

"You ok? You started leaning forward, and I had to grab you before you fell."

"I'm… fine. I just saw something. I think it was when the EMTs found us like you said they did." I turned to face him. His hands were still on my waist. I looked into his face, and our eyes locked. He leaned closer to me, and for the first time, I didn't pull away. I never realized how green his eyes were. They were like… A lush green prairie that went on for eternity… Then, I heard something that made the hair on my arms rise.

"Did you hear that?" I asked.

"Hear what?" A long hiss issued around us. I whipped my head around to see where it was coming from. It came from deep down…

Beneath us.

"Get out of the way!" I screamed.

Chapter 29

Oliver - Sunset

Malice erupted from the opened chasm with dirt and rock flying in every direction. I yelled in shock as Cora pushed me to the ground, and out of the corner of my eye, I saw her raise a hand in the air, creating a gigantic golden shield to protect us from the debris. Malice began to fly over our heads, circling like a vulture. He looked down at us and roared in laughter. His form was now more distinctive than ever. Malice's body was covered in the magenta-black goo, and his body was like a serpent, coiling and writhing in the sky. He had torn, scaly wings and black obsidian horns that seemed to glow an eerie purple. Cora glared up at Malice as if he was the most disgusting thing in the world. The sky slowly turned blood red and the sun turned as black as night, even though it was still bright outside.

"Malice has become so powerful that we can see him clearly without him being obscured to look like smoke. If we don't stop him, he will escape his domain and destroy the world!"

"We can do this," I said. I got up and unstrapped the staff from my back. It began to glow brightly. Malice dove down as fast as a hawk. He slammed right into the shield and roared. Malice continued banging into Cora's shield. She gasped and slid backward as if an invisible force had pushed her back as she kept trying to hold the shield to protect us.

"I can't hold it much longer!" Malice whammed into the shield again, and a long crack appeared in it, stretching across one side. Cora slid another few inches backward, her face contorted in pain.

"Just hang on for one more second, Cora." I said. Malice reared back, sucking in all the air around him. Then, he blew a jet of black fire straight at the shield. Cora slid another few inches backwards from its force.

"He's... Too... Strong..."

"Just one more second. . ." I just needed her to wait for the right moment, and that's when that perfect moment arrived. Malice stopped blowing the fire and paused.

"Now!" Cora lowered her hand, and the shield disappeared. I raised the spear high over my head and threw the spear right at Malice's head. It shattered on impact, and I froze in horror. I looked at Cora, and her face looked as shocked as mine.

"Uhhh. Cora? Is that supposed to happen?"

"No," Cora squeaked. Malice hissed, raising his tail like a scorpion about to strike. Cora gasped, "Oliver, get out of the way!" Malice slashed his tail down, and I dove to the side, landing hard on the ground. Cora did a backflip, his tail missing her by an inch. I got up and started running toward Cora when a black magenta sphere formed around me, trapping me inside, filling with black powder all around me. I covered my mouth, trying not to breathe it in, but I succumbed to the lack of oxygen. I breathed the powder in, and I instantly regretted it. My body felt as if it was on fire. I could feel my bones as if they were splintering inside me and slowly turning into dust. My insides were as hot as lava, slowly melting me from the inside out. I screamed in pain like I've never screamed before and collapsed.

"Oliver!" Cora's cry was so drawn out that it seemed to echo forever, even longer than my scream. She ran toward me but was thrown backward by a force emanating from the sphere. She looked helplessly at me as I continued to breathe in the powder that was slowly killing me. Cora turned to see Malice, who was shrinking down to about the size of a small house. When he spoke, a low hiss issued from all around us.

"Give up, Cora," he rasped, slithering a few feet closer to Cora. "I am stronger than you've ever seen me before. I know all of your moves. I will win."

"Never!" Cora yelled at him.

"Have it your way then." Malice flicked his tail and I could only see darkness. Then, a stabbing pain went through me as if a knife had been plunged into my chest. I yelled again in pain. I looked to see a glob of magenta-black goo where the pain had been on my chest. Looking back up, I saw Cora watching helplessly as I slowly felt myself beginning to die.

CHAPTER 30

❖

CORA - THE FINAL BATTLE

I flew backwards and hit my head against a stone wall. I tried getting up but stumbled. I clutched the wall with one hand and felt the back of my head with my hand. When I drew back my hand, blood glistened on my fingertips. In front of me, Malice laughed.

"Admit it, Cora," Malice said, slithering toward me. "I won this battle. You and your friends are no match for me. Bow to me, Cora... or I will destroy you and every last one of your pathetic protectors."

"Don't listen to him, Cora!" Oliver cried, trying to get up; he stood for a few moments then collapsed onto the ground. The magenta-black goo was already covering his entire chest and slowly creeping its way around his legs, arms, and neck.

"Enough!" Malice hissed. He flicked his tail, and Oliver let out a terrible scream, then fell silent. I called out his name, but he didn't respond. *He's dying! And there's nothing I can do.* I ran once more toward Oliver, but Malice flicked his tail and hit me. I flew backwards and collapsed onto the ground. I tried getting up but gasped in pain as I felt two of my ribs crack. Hair covered my face so Malice couldn't see me.

"Cora, be honest with yourself..." I crawled forward a few inches before collapsing again, gasping and groaning in pain. "You. Are. Alone."

Silence.

I closed my eyes, and I felt a tear trickle down my cheek. I pictured my mother, looking down at me smiling. "You're special, Cora," she said. "Never forget that." Then I remembered the dragon and how Delphi's voice had spoken to me. "I have waited eons for this day to come," she had said. "I could never be more proud of a descendant." I opened my eyes and clenched my fists. My hands began to glow golden and got brighter and brighter.

"No." I staggered to my feet and began to walk forward. The farther I walked, the stronger I felt. I could feel my power flowing through my veins, more powerful than before. My body felt as if I could move a mountain. I felt my feet leave the ground as gold and green streaks of light swirled around me, encasing me in a golden-green sphere. Something emerald green shot out of my chest. It was wispy like a ghost. The thing rose higher and higher, its form becoming clearer and clearer until it became a form of a dragon. It roared loudly, and it began to slowly circle me, protecting me from harm. Green, ghostlike wings formed on my back, and dragon horns grew on my head. "I am Cora. Daughter of Emily and Herald and descendant of the elemental goddess of the sun, Delphi." My voice rang through the air. When I spoke, I could hear a faint roar like the dragon. "I am different from the other descendants, and I'm not alone! Let Oliver go! I brought him here, and he does not need to be killed. A descendant of Delphi was destined to destroy you. He won't! So let him go, and we can finish this once and for all!"

Malice hesitated. For once, his body language made him look terrified.

"Let him go, Malice," I ordered, staring into his worried face. "Let. Him. Go." Malice snarled. The sphere around Oliver disappeared and so did the goo on his chest. Oliver got up, a little shaken. I waved my hand toward him, and a golden sphere encased him, protecting him from further harm.

"Cora! Let me out. I can help!" I looked into his eyes for a moment.

"I'm sorry, Oliver." I looked away, back at Malice, glaring at him. "I won't let anyone else get hurt." I raised my right hand, and a long, golden katana made of sunlight formed. It glowed as bright as the sun. Malice drew back slightly as if scared. Then he smiled.

"Let's even the odds, shall we?" I watched as Malice shrank down to my size and his form changed until standing in front of me was a teenage boy. He had greasy black hair. His eye sockets were empty like a black void, and his skin was covered in black matter. He held a long, obsidian axe and wore obsidian armor. As he laughed, long fangs that were a milky white showed.

"I'm tired of playing your games, Malice." I spun my sword through the air, and it came slashing down in a wide arch.

"Let's finish this," Malice snarled. I flew right at him. Our weapons collided with each other, sending a blast of pure energy into the air. It sent Malice sailing backwards. I flew after him. I whipped my hand through the air and sent a beam of light at him. Malice blocked it with his axe and sent a jet of black fire straight at my face. The dragon surrounding me extended a wing and blocked the fire. I continued to slash, kick, and parry. I was so fluent in my attacks that I was a mix of limbs and sword.

"You fight well with your ancestors' power, Cora," Malice hissed. "But give up. You're just wasting time."

"I'LL NEVER QUIT!" I yelled. I slashed downward, but Malice hooked his axe on my sword and with the force of a bomb, I crashed to the ground, missing the chasm by mere feet. He dove down, but I rolled away just in time. I swiped my hand through the air and a beam of light blasted Malice into the museum wall. Malice got up, his face looked shocked and tired. He snarled malevolently and transformed into his original form.

"I've had enough of this." As Malice soared into the air, hundreds of sharp knives that glowed magenta appeared and surrounded him. He leaned back, about to strike, then dove right at me. I raised my right hand high into the air, ready to give the final blow, and a streak of light shot right at Malice's face. I closed my eyes, ready for the impact...

But nothing happened.

I opened my eyes, looking around. Time had somehow stopped. As I looked at the world around me, I saw one of Malice's knives only one centimeter away from my left shoulder, right above my heart. *What's going on? How can this be?*

"Oh my gosh..." I muttered to myself.

"I always knew you could do it." I jumped in shock, summoned a ball of light in my hand, and whipped around. My body became numb in shock.

"Mother?" My mother was standing there, smiling. Her long, red hair was down and she was wearing the same beautiful green dress she wore when she died. There was a faint, glowing outline around her. Mother opened her arms, and I ran to hug her. "I missed you, Cora. We all have."

"What do you mean?" I turned around and gasped in shock. Nick, Kane, William, Luke, Lilly, Grace, Tyler, Doctor Johnson, and Delphi appeared behind my mother. All of them had wide smiles on their faces.

"You are a true descendant of Delphi, Cora," my mother said, "None of our ancestors could have done what you have today."

"We are all so proud of you," Kane said, smiling. I continued to look at them, trying to comprehend what was going on. Then, only one reasonable explanation occurred to me. I was dead. *The final memory was the moment before you'd die, but why didn't I look like them? With a faint outline surrounding my body?* I looked around at where Oliver stood. His face looked scared and desperate as one of his shoulders came in contact with the side of the shield, trying to break free.

"So..." I said, not looking back at the others. "What happens now?"

"You get to come home," Delphi said, her voice as soft as rain. I walked up to Oliver and placed a hand on the shield. I couldn't just leave Oliver and our friends! We've gone through so much together!

"But what if I want to stay?" I asked. "Do I have a choice?"

"Well, one is that you stay here," Delphi began, "fight Malice for another few years as his evil continues to spread or..."

"You can come with us and restore peace to Crystal Falls and everyone would be safe, just like you've always wanted!" Grace said, running up and smiling at me. "Then we can be together again!" I placed a hand on her head, thinking about how wonderful it would be to be reunited with my family. Then I looked up at Delphi.

"But either way, would I die?" Delphi paused for a moment and then nodded, her expression turning to sadness. I watched as Tyler walked forward and hugged me as if nothing had happened, like he never died. "Tyler," I said. "I'm so sorry that you died. It's my fault. I should have saved you."

"Hey, it's not your fault," he said, letting go of me and looking me straight in the eye. "It was my choice to go back and try to save the kid, not yours. You would have done the same thing if you were me."

"You barely know me though... but you're right I would've." I looked around at all of them. *What if I did stay*? But I knew that it wasn't possible. Finally, I sighed in defeat as I remembered Delphi's words:

"Sometimes, the hardest choice you have to make is the one that will help you succeed in your journey."

"I know what I have to do." I walked back to the place where I stood before I saw my mother. I turned back to look at Oliver one last time. "Goodbye, Oliver," I croaked, a tear rolling down my cheek. Then I added,"I wish we could've had more time together."

I stretched out my hand as high as it could, as if I was reaching for the stars, my shaking palm faced Malice's, malevolent stare. I looked at him, knowing that he was the last thing I'd ever see. Then with a loud warrior cry, Malice barreled toward me as he let out a loud roar...

Then there was silence.

I could hear children laughing and people talking merrily. The smell of flowers and grass filled my nostrils, and when I opened my eyes, I saw a world I had never seen before.

"Welcome home, Cora," my mother whispered in my ear.

Chapter 31

—— ※ ——

Oliver - A Final Goodbye

The world around me exploded in a flash of golden and purple light. I flew backwards as Cora's shield disappeared from the light. I heard a yell and a loud roar before I fell back, cracking my head on a block of stone, blacking out. When I woke up, I saw the yellow sun shining brightly in a pale blue sky above me. The chaos from Malice slowly disintegrated around me as everything turned back to normal. I got up, excited and relieved to know that it was finally over.

"Malice. He's gone. Crystal Falls is safe! Cora, we did it! We-" I turned around in the direction of where Cora was standing moments before. Malice had disappeared...

But Cora...

"No... No. No. No. No. No. No..." Cora was laying on her side, her limbs sprawled out in different angles like a broken doll.

"Cora!" I leapt over rubble and ran around hundreds of black knives that were lodged into the ground. I knelt down next to Cora and rolled her over so her face was towards the sky. Her eyes were closed like she was sleeping. Half of her face and neck was plagued by purple veins that curled their way up from a black knife that was lodged in Cora's left shoulder. Blood was splattered everywhere. I tried to reach for the knife, but some kind of force pushed my hand away. I clung to Cora's limp body and shook her lightly in my arms.

"Cora, stay with me, ok? If you can hear me, say something." She didn't move. I could feel my eyes beginning to fill with tears and my throat stung. Suddenly, I heard Racheal, Harper, Fin, and Cyrus running from the entrance of the garden. Racheal gasped.

"Oh, no!"

"Cora!"

"We're too late," Harper said mournfully. Fin rushed forward and knelt down next to me. He picked up one of Cora's limp wrists and felt for her pulse. After a moment, his face fell, and he looked at me.

"We can save her, right?" I pleaded, my voice cracking. "There has to be a way."

"I'm sorry," Fin said, "there is nothing we can do." I heard Harper and Racheal crying behind me. Cyrus walked up to Fin and I as he looked down at Cora. Fin let go of Cora's hand and lowered his head. I knelt there, silently. My brain was numb. I couldn't think. All I could do was look at the locket she had shown me before the battle started. It was the only thing that had not been covered in blood. I unlatched it from her neck and put it into my pocket.

"Oliver!?!" I whipped around to see who said my name. Mom and Dad both stood there, their expressions full of shock. They looked around at the destruction and then at Cora's dead body.

"Oh, sweetie."

"Mom! Dad!" I didn't care that my friends were watching, or that I looked like a little child as I ran to my parents and hugged them as tight as I could. I cried as only one thought kept circling in my mind: *Cora was gone, and there was no way to bring her back.*

❧❧❧❧❧ ❧❧❧❧❧

I never really thought about how fortunate I was to be who I am. I can speak, breathe, walk, run, laugh, smile, play sports, et cetera. But most of all, I have never fully appreciated being alive and being with my family and friends.

Cora reminded me of that.

For the past few days, Racheal, Harper, Cyrus, Fin, our parents, and I had been planning Cora's funeral, making preparations and finding a place to bury her. In the end, we finally found this beautiful place up a hill about two miles away from the town church that looked out to the ocean where Crystal Falls was said to have been first seen by travelers on a boat.

Everyone wore black, including Harper, who usually never wears it. She wore a long black dress that reached the floor with a silver belt buckled around her waist. She was holding three yellow water lilies in her hand. Her eyes looked red as if she had cried all night. Racheal was wearing a metallic black sequined dress that stopped just above the knees, and she wore black boots with silver spikes on the sides. Her hair was down, and through my teary eyes, I could see her face had a couple of tears trickling down. Fin, Cyrus, and I all wore the same black formal attire with white button up shirt and black ties.

At the church, it was only me, my friends, our parents, and the priest surrounding Cora's body. The coffin we chose was made of Santos Mahogany with golden paint outlining the edges of the wood. The symbol of Cora's royal family was carved into the top of the lid, and white silk sheets encased the inside of the coffin with a soft pillow where Cora's head rested. Cora, who had never been one to take a break, lay still and unmoving in the coffin. Her chocolate colored hair was washed and entwined with golden silk. She wore a long sleeved, beautiful white silk dress that covered her feet. Her arms were positioned to where her hands lay still on her stomach, holding the little music box that she had taken when we went back in time. Her eyes were closed, and her mouth was shut. Besides the small cuts, bruises, and the knife that was still protruding from her shoulder, she looked almost relaxed. As if she had finally found peace in the world. No one spoke, knowing that if we did, we'd all start to cry again. The priest droned on about Cora and her life story, at least everything that we'd told him about, and when it was done, he closed the lid of the coffin and gestured for eight men who volunteered to carry the coffin to come forward. They carefully picked it up and began to walk to the exit of the church and outside to the hearse. We all followed.

"I'm surprised that no one came to the funeral," Harper said in a shaky voice.

"They didn't know Cora as well as we did," Cyrus contradicted. "I guess it's not their obligation to say goodbye."

"Cyrus is right," I agreed, though my voice sounded like I was speaking in a hoarse whisper. "We didn't ask people to come and say goodbye. Sure, they knew about it, but they would've been here if they..." But my sentence was cut off as the church doors opened to reveal not ten but at least ten thousand people flooding the mainstreet that stretched its way all across the town of Crystal Falls. Because it was sunset, every man, woman, elder, and child was carrying a candle that flickered in the slight breeze. In the front of the crowd stood Chief Ansel, Chieftess Neenah, Prince Dakota, Princess June, Princess Lara, and Chayton. Behind them hovered Daemon, his expression filled with remorse.

As we walked down the church stairs, everyone knelt or bowed their heads before Cora's coffin as it passed like it was the Holy Grail. The coffin was placed into the hearse that drove slowly down the road toward Cora's final resting place. Everyone followed after it, some people were humming songs or crying.

"The entire town is here," Fin whispered.

"Why would they do such a thing?" I asked. "They barely knew her."

"Yes, but Oliver," Rahceal said, "Look at all Cora has done for us. She's taught us things that most of us didn't even know about with her family. Plus, she protected half the town from Malice's attack and sacrificed herself to save everyone."

"We came to give our respects to the Princess," said Prince Dakota, trying to give us a comforting smile.

We walked for what seemed like an hour before we arrived at the top of the hill. A rectangular hole was dug at the peak of the hill where Cora's coffin was to be buried. Everyone then got in a line and one by one knelt down in front of Cora's coffin, placing a hand on it. After a long time, it was finally our turn. We each followed after one another, kneeling and saying our goodbyes. When it was my turn, I knelt down and placed both my right hand and forehead onto Cora's coffin.

"Cora," I said, barely in a whisper. "I'm so sorry..." My voice broke before I could finish what I was going to say. I got shakily to my knees and returned back to where my friends and family now stood, my breathing becoming shallow as I tried to hold back tears. A small, warm gust of wind whisked through the air and around everyone, swirling leaves and giving me a warm, calming sensation throughout my body. It made me realize that even though Cora had left this world, she was safe and finally with her family.

And that was all that mattered.

OLIVER - TWO YEARS LATER

I walked down a long pathway leading up to the castle ruins. Even though half of it was destroyed, it was still open for tours to remind everyone of what happened two years ago. When I opened the door, four people stood there with their backs facing me. Harper, Rachael, Fin, and Cyrus were looking up at a large statue of Cora. Cora had her hand raised to the sky, palming facing up. Her hair was thrown back as if an invisible wind carried it, her face full of determination as she faced her foe.

When the door thudded behind me, my friends turned to face me. Fin had sideburns and wore a nice suit and tie as well as a ruby ring on his ring finger. He was holding hands with Racheal, who had cut her hair super short and flipped it to one side. She wore spiked bracelets and a crop top that had a bunch of miniature skulls on it. She, too, wore a ruby ring wrapped around her ring finger. Cyrus had a goatee and wore a t-shirt and jeans. Harper had dyed her hair a deep red, and she was wearing a white dress and high heels.

"Hey man!" Cyrus said, smiling at me. "Long time, no see!"

"It's nice to see you again, Oliver," Rachael said, hugging me.

"It's nice to see you guys again, too, and I'm glad you got my message."

Fin looked back up into the statue's face.

"I can't believe how long it's been since we've seen each other."

"Yeah, time flies," Cyrus agreed.

"Well, we all just saw each other a month ago for Racheal and Fin's engagement party, " Harper added. Racheal laughed a little before going quiet. We all stood there, silent for a moment. It felt as if another two years seemed to pass by us. Then Cyrus broke the silence.

"So, what's wrong, Oliver? You sounded worried when you called us."

"Well... I've been having these dreams." Immediately, their expressions turned from curiosity to concern.

"What kind of dreams?" Cyrus asked.

"I'm not sure, but last night, I saw Cora."

"Woah, woah, woah, wait! You saw Cora?" Racheal asked, astounded.

"Explain," Fin said, eagerly. I took a deep breath and looked at the ground.

"This time, the room was dark. A spotlight was on her. She was chained up and crying."

"What happened then?" Cyrus asked.

"Well, she tried talking to me."

"Did she say anything that might have explained why she was chained?" Harper asked.

"She tried, but she couldn't speak. I could only make out one word."

"What was it?" Racheal asked.

"Help."

Suddenly, the lights flickered and went out. Harper screamed in terror. I pulled out my phone and tried turning it on, but nothing happened. I felt Racheal grab my wrist and squeeze it so hard that I yelped in pain. She let go instantly.

"Sorry!"

"I think someone is nearby," Fin said. "We're not alone." A low growl rose around us. We squinted through the dark, trying to see where it was coming from.

"Look out!" Rachael, Fin, Cyrus, and Harper fell on top of me before I could react. We scrambled up and continued to look around. Out of the corner of my eye, I saw a figure of a woman land in front of us about twenty feet away. The woman glowed a faint magenta, illuminating her figure and the room. She had pale gray skin and long, dark black hair that seemed to float around her. Her outfit was entirely black with golden lining. She carried a long obsidian double axe that glistened in the magenta light. Her eyes were black with purple pupils. Purple markings curved and twisted their way along half of her face like vines. She hissed at us, and I shivered as goosebumps rose all over my skin. She looked very familiar. I looked closely at a gash in her left shoulder that was about the size of a knife...

"No way..." I said, my expression breaking into realization.

"What?" Cyrus said. He pulled out a pocket knife and flipped it open. I walked a step forward, closer to the woman.

"Oliver! What are you doing?" I ignored Rachael's warning and took one step closer.

"Cora?" Cora opened her mouth and fangs glistened brightly. A forked tongue flicked as a long hiss left her mouth. She raised her axe high into the air with one hand, and conjured magenta-black fire in the other. Out of the corner of my eye, I saw Harper take two steps back.

"This isn't good."

ACKNOWLEDGMENTS

A special thanks to my family, my best friend and cover illustrator Lara Funnell, my editor William Brydon, my friends, my teachers, my followers on social media, my voice over friends, Brent Miller, the NINJAGO community, and everyone who has encouraged and supported me throughout this journey. You were my inspiration and motivation to continue doing my dream.

ABOUT THE AUTHOR

Violet Noel was born in Michigan and moved to Oshkosh, Wisconsin at a very young age. At the age of seven, she joined a musical theater group called JuBriCoSa and from there fell in love with the theater, singing, and the art of creating a story. She won a Junior Thespian Award for acting at age 12. She started her writing journey by writing various fan fictions, including submitting an entire show series to the writer group for consideration. Her latest work, The Legend of Crystal Falls, is one her own creation. She hopes you enjoy it and that it inspires young readers to reach for their own dreams.

Made in the USA
Monee, IL
13 December 2022

21417704R00131